The ABCs of Dinkology:

Life

AE Stueve

EAB Publishing - Omaha

THE ABCS OF DINKOLOGY: LIFE PUBLISHED BY EAB PUBLISHING (2014)

COPYRIGHT EAB PUBLISHING 2014.

THE ABCS OF DINKOLOGY: LIFE TEXT COPYRIGHT AE STUEVE.

COVER AND INTERIOR PAGE ART COPYRIGHT CHRIS SMITH.

FIRST EDITION PUBLISHED AS THE ABCS OF DINKOLOGY BY WSC PRESS (2012).

ISBN 10: 0692300600

ISBN 13: 9780692300602

FOR MORE INFORMATION ABOUT EAB PUBLISHING VISIT www.EABPublishing.com.

THE NEXT VOLUME OF MAX DINKMAN'S STORY, THE ABCS OF DINKOLOGY: TIME IN-

BETWEEN, IS NOW AVAILABLE FROM EAB PUBLISHING.

FOLLOW MAX'S EXPLOITS AT WWW.FACEBOOK.COM/THEABCSOFDINKOLOGY.

THIS BOOK IS FOR MY PARENTS WHO SOMEHOW MADE

ME A WRITER.

AE STUEVE

FOR MY BROTHER, MIKE, WHO FIRST INSPIRED ME TO

PICK UP A PENCIL AND SCRATCH OUT A MESS OF A

SCENE IN EMULATION OF HIS GIFT.

AND FOR MY FRIEND, DEREK A, WHOSE OWN

BIZARRELY BEAUTIFUL CREATIONS KEPT THAT PENCIL

BETWEEN MY FINGERS. THANK YOU BOTH.

CHRIS SMITH

Acknowledgements

First and foremost, I'd like to thank Cynthia Black, Chad Christensen, and, most importantly, my first editor, Jaclyn Pendleton, of WSC Press, also, William Kloefkorn, former Nebraska State Poet, for seeing something worth publishing in this mad mix of comic book pages, prose, trading cards, footnotes, and whatever else I thought was cool. Without these people, the first edition of *The ABCs of Dinkology* would still be languishing in my brain's sub-basement instead of being part of WSC's Kloefkorn Series.

Additionally, Chris Smith and Ernest Nathan Acosta III deserve a lion's share of acknowledgement. These two fine gentlemen turned my words into art that continually floors me. Without them, *The ABCs of Dinkology* would be a weak shadow of what it is. I am forever and always in their debt for what they've done. Also, the other artists who provided their skills for the character biography/trading cards deserve thanks. Gregg Paulsen, Michael McMahon, Kristy Edgar, and Britt Marvin have shown their artistic chops by perfectly capturing the essence of the characters within these pages.

The University of Nebraska MFA in Creative Writing program is on this list of acknowledgements as well. Specifically, Karen Gettert Shoemaker, Amy Hassinger, Mark Haskell Smith, and Trish Lear need to be named. Every other mentor, guest lecturer, and student whose insight helped turn *The ABCs of Dinkology* into something worth reading deserves thanks as well. While I am at it, the writers I have read and admire, ranging from Stan Lee to John Steinbeck get a shoutout. There are more, to be sure, but that list is too long to include here.

I must also acknowledge the entire EAB Publishing team: Tim Benson, Jeremy Morong, Britton Sullivan, Julie Rowse, Grant Campbell, Brittney Marvin, Carrie Helmberger, the irrepressible intern, Ashley Quintela and Jill Stewart, a copy editor whose eyes are clearly magic. This group of people comes together on a regular basis to produce fantastic literature. The list of EAB's publications includes the seasonal magazine *Midnight Circus* and David Atkinson's novel, *The Garden of Good and Evil Pancakes,* which *The ABCs of Dinkology* is proud to now call kin.

Naturally, it goes without saying that I must thank my family and friends, all of them and always.

Finally, thank you, dear reader, for taking a chance on the madness that is *The ABCs of Dinkology: Life* and/or *The ABCs of Dinkology: Time In-Between.* I hope you enjoy.

--AE Stueve

The ABCs of Dinkology:

Life

Lesson One: Social Studies

Sunday October 31, 1999

SUGGESTED MUSICOGRAPHY

Louis Armstrong—"What a Wonderful

World"

Red Hot Chili Peppers—"Scar Tissue"

Beck—"Bottle of Blues"

THE DINKMAN HOUSE. DAVENPORT, IA. 5:00 P.M.

MAX!

ARE YOU GOING TO EAT WITH US?

NO MOM, I TOLD YOU; I'M GOING OUT WITH LAURA.

I THOUGHT SHE WAS SUPPOSED TO BE HERE AT 4:30?

SHE WAS.

WHY DON'T YOU COME IN? YOUR DAD CAN HAND OUT CANDY.

SHE'LL BE HERE.

HOW'S YOUR ARM? DO YOU NEED MORE PAIN PILLS?

IT'S BEEN TWO MONTHS, MOM.

MY ARM'S FINE.

IF SHE ISN'T HERE IN FIFTEEN MINUTES, I WANT YOU TO COME INSIDE.

FINE.

TRICK-OR-TREAT!

HERE YOU GO.

THANKS!

AND STOP EATING ALL THE EXPENSIVE CANDY, DAMNIT!

TRICK
-OR-
TREAT!

Lately, Max Dinkman found himself imagining his world as one big comic book. There was no rhyme or reason to these brief forays into an existence of harsh, black lines, pages, panels, and word balloons, at least none he could see. However, doing so made him feel at ease when he knew, deep down, he wasn't. But as he saw his girlfriend's blue, rusted out, 1992 Honda Civic, a mean case of the bubbleguts erupted inside him that the comic book life he was living could not subdue. Laura Levinson, the older, artistic army brat who winked her way into his heart and then ran off to college, had returned. Even the thought of her name gave him goose bumps. Max took a deep breath. If there were a devil, he would gladly sell his soul to that horned beast if it meant his relationship with Laura could go back to the way it had been—before the Chicago Art Institute had stolen her away like some kind of philandering older man going through a midlife crisis.

Max let the breath out and closed his eyes, imagining he was Gambit, the Cajun mutant,[1] waiting for his love, Rogue, the Southern Belle mutant.[2] He felt stubble growing on his chin and cheeks. His jacket became a trench coat, flapping melodramatically in the wind. His fingers twitched as he flipped around the deck of playing cards he always carried to charge into deadly weapons. As she approached, he grasped for something ominous or enigmatic to say in Creole.

Laura turned into Rogue. Her short, straight hair grew into Max's favorite of all of Rogue's coifs—a long and wavy brunette mass of curls with a white stripe shooting up the middle. Her teenaged body was no longer fragile and petite; instead, she was a *woman*. Her breasts increased by at least two cup sizes, she grew a few inches taller, and her muscles appeared

---

[1] Remy LeBeau, a mutant with the ability to turn anything into a kinetic energy charged bomb, foreboding X-Man, New Orleans born and raised master thief. He has a dark and mysterious past, wears a trench coat all the time, speaks Creole, and carries a pack of playing cards with him wherever he goes. He must really exist, because you can't make stuff like that up.

[2] As of 1999, her real name is unknown, Rogue is a reformed villain and adopted daughter of super-villain, mutant Mystique, Rogue is also an X-Man. She can take the memories, mind, soul (some hypothesize), life, and/or powers of any person she touches, which makes any physical relationship with her a problem.

taut and strong beneath her green and yellow, skintight superhero uniform. Max-Gambit's mouth watered as his eyes traced the edges of her comic book curves.

Laura-Rogue flew toward him with open arms—she didn't need her Honda. Words of apology for the long absence of communication were on her bright, red comic book lips. He thought they might taste like Southern iced tea on a humid day. His mouth watered some more.

Even though it was a fantasy, Max felt a tingle in his pants he knew he would have trouble controlling. *But how can I control it?* he thought. *She's irresistible. She seduced Magneto once and he's practically a god!*[3]

Max tried to play it cool.

He stood on what became the front drive of Xavier's School for Gifted Youngsters,[4] flipping his cards. He reminded himself he was no longer the 17-year-old boy who didn't understand much of anything, especially women. He was Max-Gambit, the grizzled anti-hero. He pulled a cigar from his pocket and placed it to his lips, an indicator that the quickly approaching Laura-Rogue had better not touch him. As he did this, a pained look flashed across her face.

Hurts, doesn't it? Max-Gambit couldn't help but be a little satisfied. *I wasn't the one who cut all contact when you moved away for college.*

His cards grew heated. He could feel the kinetic energy building. The pink, bubbling power ran up his fingers in ticklish fits. Max-Gambit wasn't going to let her get close enough to talk. He was ready for an old-fashioned superhero battle. Their fists would fly. Cars would explode. The sound of every blow would echo across the state. Entire city blocks would be reduced to craters. In the end, when the fight was over and the neighborhood was nothing more than various piles of burning rubble, Laura-Rogue would try to kiss him—but she wouldn't. If she did, he could lose his powers, his mind, his life, or maybe his soul. Neither of them

---

[3] Magneto, AKA Eric Lehnsherr, AKA Magnus, AKA Max Eisenhardt, evil (some say "complicated") mutant with magnetic abilities. He once had a tryst with Rogue that lasted through "The X-Tinction Agenda," in Marvel Comics' "X" books (1990-1991).
[4] Sprawling Westchester County New York mansion home of the X-Men!

wanted that. They could never touch. They could never kiss. They could never fuck.[5]

But Laura wouldn't let Max go all the way with her because it was *never the right time*. Gambit's girlfriend at least had a legitimate excuse for not having sex—it could kill him. Unless Laura knew something Max didn't, two virgins having sex was not a recipe for death.

With that, his fantasy evaporated like a series of popping thought bubbles.

What if Laura isn't a virgin? What if there was only one reason all the times our foreplay never led to any playplay? What if I just suck at all this stuff? Why do I suck? Isn't this one of those things that's supposed to be hardwired into my genetic makeup? "Shit," Max breathed as Laura's car stopped in front of his driveway. She didn't turn off the engine. "Shit," he said again, waving, smiling, and acting like the pathetic loser his shirt claimed he was. A cloud of pale smoke hovered around the car as Max walked toward it.

"Happy Halloween," he said. "You're late."

Laura didn't respond. She put the car in park and lit a cigarette. "Sorry Max," she whispered, then raised her voice so he could hear her from behind the rolled-up window, "I can't go out tonight."

The way she said it, with her lips wrapped around the cigarette, her voice smooth and at ease, stunned him.

"Why?" he asked. He hoped he didn't sound like a whiny teenager, but knew damn well that was exactly how he sounded.

Before Laura could answer or turn her head, Moses' loud bark sounded from inside the house. They both jumped.

Max spun around, aggravated, and shouted, "Shut up, Moses!" He figured she couldn't hear him, or that she wouldn't obey even if she could, but he had to do something. He needed to take his attention away from the

---

[5] Actually . . . as of *Uncanny X-Men #348* (October 1997) thanks to some temporary power neutering, it seems Rogue and Gambit had an opportunity to at least kiss— whether or not anything else happened between #348 and #349 is an oft-debated topic at comic book shops, conventions, and moms' basements all over the country.

beautiful girl parked in front of his house, refusing to go out with him tonight. This beautiful girl who had spent the summer with him, but who had now moved on, leaving him here, alone.

Laura rolled down the passenger side window. "That dog never did like me," she sighed, and leaned over the seat to smile at Max, her unreasonably white teeth dazzling from behind slightly parted pink lips and a fog of lingering smoke.

Max felt his world fall out from under him as her dark eyes focused on his. "Why?" Max asked again.

"Why doesn't your dad's dog like me? How the hell should I know?"

Max noticed her voice was silky and heavier than it had been the last time he had seen her, as if moving away and going to college had matured and sophisticated her to levels he would never attain.

"What?" Max asked, shaking his head. "What? No. Why can't you go out tonight? You promised."

"I just can't," she replied, her tone blunt. Then she dug through the massive black leather purse on her car's soda-can-encrusted floorboard.

The finality in her voice made Max feel like an afterthought, a nuisance, and anger seared through his body, causing his cheeks to flare red and his hands and forehead to sweat. "What do you mean?"

"Here, take this," she interrupted, and handed an envelope through the opened window. "It'll explain everything."

Max backed up and shook his head. "No," he snapped. "Whatever you've got to say to me, say it to my face. I don't want your stupid letter." The cold air began to nibble his exposed skin. He flinched as the breeze picked up.

"Come on, Max," Laura insisted.

"No."

Laura took a deep breath and held it in for a moment before sitting up straight. She looked down at the letter now in her lap. "Fine," she whispered, her voice soft and strained. She turned the engine off and reluctantly stepped out. "We'll talk. But we have to make it quick."

Max tried to remain firm, but couldn't resist observing the way she moved as she shut the door and walked around to the front of her car. Laura's eyes were captured by a hypnotic beauty that was everything but Max. Her motions were sleek, practiced. She was, despite the oversized clothes and college swagger, the girl he loved. Her face was flushed from the cold, and as she climbed onto the hood, Max thought he saw her shiver. His anger began to thaw. He sat next to her, anxious, and doled out candy to a few trick-or-treaters.

Laura twirled the letter in her hands.

"Okay. Talk."

She glanced toward the street, quiet.

"Come on Laura," Max said, impatient, "Tell me what's going on."

"I wish you'd just let me give you the letter," she replied.

Max placed a hand on her shoulder. He didn't know how much more of her resistance he could take. "Seriously Laura, what's wrong?"

Some kids in costumes walked up to the car and begged for candy. Max gave them handfuls without looking.

"I'm waiting . . . ."

"Max . . . ."

"Why can't you just tell me?" Frustration oozed from his mouth but he tried to compose himself. "You know, whatever it is . . ." he whispered, sincere, "You can tell me."

Laura moved away from him then, just enough so his hand fell off her shoulder. Max blinked.

She took two big drags of her cigarette and flicked the butt into the street before turning to face him, her features cold and secretive, and said, "I'm gay."

Max remembered the cheesy movies his mom used to watch on Saturday afternoons when he was a kid, and how time always stopped when lovers met for the first time. It was a magical moment of romanticized purity, and though he would have trouble admitting it, those moments always made him feel hopeful. Now, as the world ground so loudly he could hear the gears popping and the shafts cracking, time literally came to an unhealthy stop. Her words inflicted irrevocable damage to his insides, and he knew those movies were liars.

"What?" he gawked.

"I'm gay."

" . . . What?"

"I'm gay, Max. Just . . . I'm gay."

Max felt his heart implode. "Please!" he blurted, wild, his voice tangled in confusion and despair. "Please . . ." he continued, his mouth suddenly dry, "stop saying that." He leaned forward, woozy as the world started spinning again.

Laura wiped tears from her cheeks, sniffling. "And that's not all."

"What? What the fuck else are you going to tell me?" he asked, and though he meant the words to come out angry, they sounded sad and deflated.

"Trick or treat!" more costumed children giggled and held out their bags while middle-aged mothers stood a few feet away, giving sidelong glances at Max, his broken arm, his dazed expression, and his massive bowl of candy.

"Here take it all and leave me the hell alone!" Max yelled, dropping the bowl to the ground and ignoring the children as they ignored his anger and darted for the pile of candy in his driveway.

Laura hopped off the hood and slid one long sleeve over her eyes, smearing wet mascara across her face.

"Wait—" Max followed and caught her by her shoulder as she opened the driver's door. "Please, what else did you want to tell me?"

"Max," she said as new tears swelled up. Laura closed her eyes, "Max, you're gay too. You just haven't realized it yet." Then she handed him the letter, got into her car, and left without another word.

Dumbfounded, Max watched her car disappear around the corner at the end of his block. Memories of her, blotted by dejection, bombarded his mind. As the streetlights buzzed and flickered on, Max made a tight fist with his good hand, and yelled, "I'm not gay!"

After taking a few shaky breaths, face tingling, he bent down to pick up the empty candy bowl. "I wish there was more candy," he whimpered, looking up into the blackened sky.

Snow Day

SUGGESTED MUSICOGRAPHY

Ennio Morricone—"The Ecstasy of Gold"

After a fitful sleep of half-remembered dreams brought on by a combination of seeing Laura, reading her letter, and munching on a pile of candy into the wee hours of the night, Max went to school in a daze. Classes whirled by with no real meaning. He talked to his friends and even answered a teacher's question or two, but everything was clouded. Sadness and anger at Laura's words—and fear that she might be right—invaded his every thought.

Max had always been one to see the attractiveness of men as well as women. There were times when Laura and he would go to the mall, sit on a bench, and point out the beautiful and the ugly passersby, male and female. It was one of their favorite pastimes. Thinking back, it seemed obvious she was gay.

Was it obvious I was? I can't be. My dick never got hard for a dude, even a hot dude . . . did it? Comic books are full of mostly buff dudes. I sure as shit read a lot of those. I'm a poet too. There's lots of gay poets.[6] Interview with a Vampire *is one of my favorite movies.*[7] *There's all kinds of hot dudes in that.* His mind focused on the possibility he might be gay all day until all he wanted to do was smoke some weed and forget about it.

Then the snowstorm hit.

When the final bell rang, Max walked out of North High into a barrage of moshing snowflakes and sleet. One of his best friends, Paul Nicholson, and his little sister, Maddy, were with him. Max always likened the three of them to DC Comic's[8] Big Three. When they were together, they were the mightiest heroes in the DC canon: Batman, Superman, and Wonder Woman.[9] But a serious snowstorm on the first of November was too much, even for them.

---

[6] William S. Burroughs, Lord Byron, Mark Doty, Allen Ginsberg, Langston Hughes, Frank O'Hara and Oscar Wilde . . . just to name a few.

[7] Max had been made fun of on more than one occasion for liking a film with clear homosexual overtones. Brad Pitt, Tom Cruise, Antonio Banderas, and Christian Slater all together in one movie? What gay man wouldn't want to see that?

[8] Detective Comics. Yes, that's what it stands for.

[9] Max, of course, is Batman. You can figure out the rest.

"What the fuck?" Maddy said, shoving her hands into her pink puffy coat. Her bedazzled purple puppy purse slid down her shoulder to dangle at her wrist.

"Yeah," Paul repeated, "what the fuck?"

Max shrugged. He reached into his back pocket to touch the letter from Laura. "Let's go. I have to work tonight and I want to get high first."

"You should skip work and we should all go to Taylor's," Maddy said.

Taylor O'Grady was Maddy's closest friend. She had a massive crush on Max since as long as he could remember and he never understood why.

Max knew Maddy was hinting Taylor wanted to see him. "God," he groaned, "no."

"Oh come on, Max. She's great. You know you like her."

"It doesn't matter how great she is, I have to go to work."

"Shit," Paul said, shuffling on out of the sibling rivalry and looking back. "I'd call in sick. They already closed the mall, so I'm not working tonight, sucker."

"Yeah Max, come on, call in sick. It's not like Shop More's going to be busy. Let Scott handle it all, he works tonight too, right?" Maddy jogged through the drifting snow to catch up with Paul.

Max laughed at the idea of his friend, Scott Lopez, manning the dairy cooler. "Yeah," he said, "Scott works tonight, but he spends too much time combing his hair to do what I do."

Paul thought about that for a moment, pausing. "Yeah," he said, "I guess you're right."

"And anyway, I kind of need the money," Max hollered over the howling wind. He looked out at the parking lot; it reminded him of "The Battle of Hoth."[10] There were immobile vehicles everywhere, some spitting out fumes, others sitting silently, caked with frost. Red faces, struggling bodies, and snow abounded. *If there were laser beams flying through the sky and nameless rebels being blown into the air, it* would *be just like Hoth,*

---

[10] This battle takes place in the seminal sci-fi classic, George Lucas' oft imitated, never duplicated *Star Wars Episode V: The Empire Strikes Back.*

Max thought. He pulled his hand from his back pocket, wrapped his left arm around his chest, and shivered.

"What do you need money for, anyway?" Paul asked. "Comics? How expensive could they be? It isn't like you buy anything else."

"Uh, well, gas for driving you guys everywhere."

"Whatever, dude. You may have to pay for gas, but hanging out with us keeps you cool. I'd say that's a fair trade."

"Are you serious right now? Because—"

"Guys . . ." Maddy interjected, her voice shaky and afraid. "Look who's here."

Jack Ford appeared out of the snow like an apparition, a few feet in front of Maddy. He was grimacing, his deep-set eyes shining with the kind of hatred Max knew only a person of Jack's mentality and stature could pull off. He was a savage Wendigo coming out of the woods, hungry to feast on the always outmatched Canadian super-group, Alpha Flight.[11]

"Max," Jack said. The word came out simultaneously as a challenge and a cry of disgust. His voice didn't have to compete with the winds. "I've been waiting for you."

"I'm right here," Max snapped back, shocking himself with the instant anger in his voice. But there was something more shocking; he wasn't afraid.

Jack Ford, revved up on testosterone, had been Max's own personal nightmare for years. He thought of Jack as his antithesis, his archenemy. He was Max's sister Melissa's on-again/off-again boyfriend, and the father of her unborn baby. He was also bigger than Max, meaner than Max, and had been craving for an excuse to beat Max up.

Max usually avoided Jack out of an animalistic sense of self-preservation—but today was the wrong day. Jack's convenient appearance outside of the school forced all of Max's survival instincts to the rear of his mind.

---

[11] Wendigo is not only an awesome Native American myth, it is a creepy Marvel Comics villain as well who has battled several mainstream Marvel characters, including Alpha Flight, Canada's answer to American superheroes. Yeah, they are as cool as they sound.

I don't even care. I'm just going to fucking punch him and see what happens, Max thought, stepping forward. "What do you want?" He could hear the song from *The Good, the Bad, and the Ugly*[12] playing as his anger rolled around inside him like hurricane waves. This was going to be it—the final showdown—the point in the story where the hero faces his fears and becomes the man he always wanted to be. There was a small, illogical voice in the back of Max's head, telling him if he were to fight Jack, even if he lost, Laura might change her mind about him. He stepped closer, placing himself between Jack and Maddy. "What?" Max demanded.

Paul didn't say anything, but stood next to Max with his arms crossed over his chest. Max could tell he was trying hard to look tough, and in his black and red checkered coat, Paul almost had an angry lumberjack appearance. But with Jack standing across from them, breathing through gritted teeth, and wearing only a white Chicago Bears sweatshirt and matching baggy sweatpants, *almost* wasn't enough.

"I heard about your poem," Jack growled.

What poem? Max thought. He could see Jack's muscles ripple beneath the Bears sweatshirt; they were itching to hurt him. A twinge of familiar fear mixed with confusion popped inside his mind. Max looked at Paul, cocked an eyebrow, and whispered, "What the hell is he talking about?"

"Shit," Paul said under his breath. "I told you not to read that out loud."

"Oh," Max gulped, "*that* poem." He had read his "tribute" to Jack in English the Friday before. Paul told him Jack would hear about it; Davenport Public Alternative School (DPAS) was only a couple blocks away, and Jack still had friends attending North High. Paul had said Jack would come seeking revenge for this affront like some kind of twisted super-villain—and here he was.

I should've listened, said Max's twinge of fright. *Why did I read that stupid fucking poem?*

---

[12] "The Ecstacy of the Dead" by Ennio Morricone—epic.

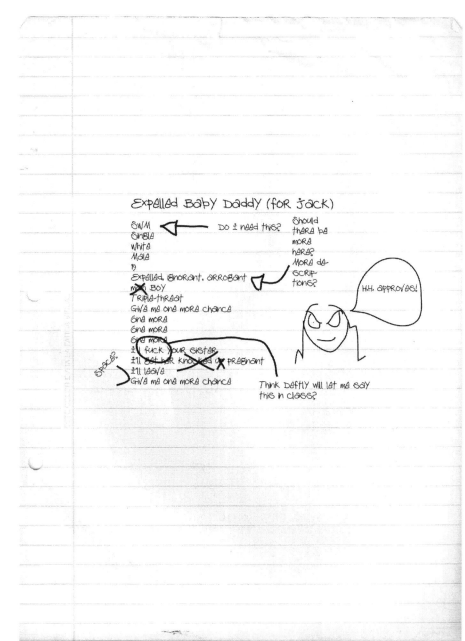

"Uh, about that . . ." Max began. The twinge of fear became a roaring in his ears.

"I'm going to kick your ass, homo!" Jack shouted.

"Fuck you!" Max recoiled, his good hand instinctively reaching for the letter in his back pocket. He noticed Jack's fists were getting bigger. He tried to ignore them, and puffed up enough courage to say, "You're not going to do anything to me." *Why did I say that?* "I'm not scared of you, Jack." *Why did I say that?*

"You should be, faggot," Jack reached across the blowing snow for Max's head. He took a fist full of Max's hair and forced his head down into the snow.

"I'm not—" Max began to argue, but a blow to his stomach knocked the wind out of him.

"Shut up!" Jack said, punching Max again.

What the fuck are his fists made of, rock? Max struggled as he lost his backpack and winter hat in the snow. He reached anxiously for Jack's arm, revulsion ripping through his veins, and embarrassed tears oozing like blood from his eyes. He was ready to fight back though, determined to show Jack he could defend himself honorably, like a Cyclops.[13] But Max's indignation evaporated as quickly as it flared. Trying to grab Jack was like trying to grab a brick wall. *I don't stand a chance.*

Max wondered if Jack spent twice as much time working out as he spent reading comic books. This was a particularly disturbing thought, since Max spent a lot of time reading comic books. Jack was like a thundering volcano, bursting with determination to prove he was a man, something Max never considered until Laura questioned his sexuality.

Paul yelled, "Let go!" and moved to help.

Jack laughed in response. With merciless speed, he swung one hard fist into Paul's gut, and sent Max's only opportunity of survival stumbling into a snowdrift.

Maddy squealed, too afraid to move.

---

[13] Scott Summers, Cyclops, the first, the consummate, X-Man. He is quiet, stoic, honest, and possesses a red optic blast that can destroy just about anything.

Shit, shit, shit. Max was panicking. Jack started pulling Max's hair out by the roots. Max thought he could hear the tiny popping sounds in his ears. *Why did I read that stupid poem? Why did I write a poem about Jack? I don't even* like *Melissa. Why do I care?* He was too frantic to conjure up an image of himself as another comic book hero. There weren't any teachers in the parking lot. Paul was still struggling to get to his feet. Maddy had turned into a statue. *Think, Max, think!* He tried to formulate a plan, but the pain registering in his head, and the way his body was wheezing through each breath made it difficult. He was cold and hot at the same time, his stomach aching from Jack's punches. All Max could see was snow.

A crowd was gathering. "Yeah!" "Go!" "Fight!" "Beat each other shitless!" The shouts echoed in Max's ears. When Ms. Deftly had asked if he wanted to share his poem with the class, he should have said no. At least she gave him a nod when he sat down—the response closest to a compliment anyone ever got from that English teacher.

Is it worth this though? Max thought as the burning pain fully hit him. He lost all the strength in his legs. They slid on the wet pavement, falling out from underneath him. His arm banged uselessly against Jack as his attacker's grip tightened. Max stumbled. *What should I do?* Salty tears drowned his eyes. He could hear Jack take a few quick breaths. Max tried to ready himself for a ruthless beating—but the horror of subsequent humiliation and pain was suffocating his senses. *Think, damn it, think! There has to be something!*

Then a thought occurred to Max like a magical savior at the last minute of a stupid movie. As Jack flung Max's body through the parking lot, he remembered something Melissa had said about Jack's parents and took a risk.

"Go ahead," Max spit while Jack yanked on him like a Rottweiler ripping apart a teddy bear, "kick my ass in the school parking lot. I'm sure you won't get expelled for that!"

Jack let go of Max almost as fast as he had grabbed him, sending Max crumbling to the ground. Pointing out the possibility of expulsion wasn't dignified, heroic, or tough, but it had worked. That was Jack's weakness—

his parents and their demands. He had to move out of his parents' house if he didn't graduate.

"Faggot!" Jack said, backing off while Maddy helped Paul out of the snowdrift.

"We'll see who's a fag when you get arrested, asshole!" Paul yelled as Jack stomped toward the beat-up, brown Mercury Max would have noticed and avoided if it weren't for the snow.

"I'm not a fag," Max quietly assured himself.

The small crowd dispersed now that the show was over. A horn honked somewhere behind the three of them and a blue minivan pulled up. Paul's mom's plump arm stuck out the window, waving.

"Your mom's here." Maddy waved back at the van and nudged Paul, who was helping Max up and mumbling about why he should listen to him.

"Shit, she probably doesn't trust you driving in this weather," Paul said. He waved goodbye, and told Max he would call later.

"Yeah. Thanks for the help," Max muttered.

"What was he supposed to do, get beat up too?" Maddy asked as Paul ran to his mother's van. "He did his best. You should be grateful."

"You heard that?"

Maddy rolled her eyes and sighed. "Are you okay? Did he hurt your arm?"

"Yeah—no, I'm fine." Max rubbed his head where Jack had pulled out some of his hair. His gut was still tender, but manageable. "Don't worry. He didn't touch my arm."

"How many times are you guys going to do this before he kicks your ass for real?"

"I hope a lot more. Or like . . . he just never kicks my ass."

"Are you going to tell Mel?"

"Why would I? Fuck her."

"Yeah. Mom?"

Max shrugged, "Probably not."

"Paul told me about that poem. I can't believe Deftly let you say 'fuck' in class."

"She said because it was for poetry it was cool."

"Too bad Paul isn't riding home with us." She picked up Max's backpack and hat, dusted off the snow, and handed them over. "I bet you could really use a joint now. I'm pretty sure he had some, and I *know* he feels like a jerk for getting thrown out of the fight like that. We could go to Chad's for a little bit? Scholtz has always got the green."

Chad Scholtz, the diminutive pot supplier of North High, always had weed and was one of Max's closest friends. But Max already had something to smoke, and didn't feel like seeing anyone after the beating he just received. "No, it's not a big deal. Paul gave me a joint in sixth period. I'll smoke it when I take Moses for a walk. But hey . . . I want to talk to you about something."

***

"Oh no!" Maddy's voice rang inside Max's head. Her clanging laughter bounced around his four-door Geo Metro's dented red frame like some kind of drunken town crier's manic shouts. "Laura's gay?" Maddy pounded her knee.

Max managed to keep Laura's secret through the school day, but he had to tell someone. He needed to let it out. Paul, Chad, and Scott were never options, but now that he had told his *loving* little sister, he thought their reactions might have been better.

Maddy howled. And hooted. And howled some more.

"Do you think you could tone it down some? I'm trying to drive," Max said in the vain hope Maddy would return to normal. He motioned with his finger at the snow and sleet mix pelting the street and turning into ice.

"I'm sorry, I'm sorry." She tried to settle. "I can't believe it though. Laura is gay . . . fucking rug muncher."

"Dude! Just don't tell anybody, okay?" Max asked, pounding the heating vent with his good fist.

"Shouldn't you keep your working hand on the wheel?"

"Shouldn't you not laugh at your older brother's woes?"

"'Woes,'" Maddy's obnoxious giggles returned. "Have you been reading Shakespeare? You are *so* gay!" This statement amused her so much she started to snort.

Max flinched. He hadn't told Maddy about Laura's theory regarding his sexuality. "Fuck you," he murmured. "And Shakespeare's not gay."[14]

Maddy lost all composure at this, "Maybe," she stuttered through fits of savage laughter, "maybe Laura would like to fuck me."

"God, I hate you," Max said through a sigh.

Before she could respond, the world swirled like the falling snow, twirling out of control, and her laughter gave way to screams. Max realized, too late, it was his car doing the violent dance, not the world. The steering wheel turned into a little circular gremlin, twisting against all the force in his hands.

"Shit!" Max yelled as cars flew past like two-ton bullets in a blur of white and panicked honks.

"We're going to die!" Maddy repeated until Max couldn't hear her over his own screams.

His mind told him to calm down; it was just a patch of ice on wet pavement. They were going to be fine—but his body wouldn't listen. The heating vents kicked out cold air, but sweat seeped through Max's skin up the length of his cast and out the pores on his forehead and temples. His fingers dug into the shifter. Knives stabbed his arm from inside and out. He shifted down. The Geo Metro jerked like an unbalanced washing machine. He put it in neutral. The tires spun, Ferris wheels operated by drunken carnies.

Max thought his sister was right. They were going to die.

A bigger vehicle—a garbage truck filled to the rim with rot, or a sand truck slipping ironically on the ice in front of it—was going to come along as his car spun in the middle of the four lanes of 53rd Street, and that would be that. Hopefully, he would be so splattered nobody would find the letter from Laura in his back pocket.

---

[14] Well . . . he might have been. Did you know most of those famous love sonnets were written for a dude? True fact.

Dad always says death is the last great adventure. What better time to find out if that's true than the day after I was dumped by a lesbian who told me I was gay?

More horns honked. More tires screeched. Max braced himself. His broken arm throbbed as he struggled to grip the shifter.

A curb formed a line in the ice. Max closed his eyes. A thick thud jolted his tires. He could hear Maddy crying. The car's engine died, sputtering as it slowed, and finally stopped.

"Holy shit," he gasped. Max looked at his sister. Tears were running down her cheeks. He ran his hands over his head, knocking his hat off. "We're alive . . ." He shuddered and laughed. "Tiny victories, huh?"

"Get me home," Maddy said, clutching her bedazzled purple puppy purse.

"Are you okay?"

"What the fuck was that?"

"Some ice or something, I guess."

"Shit," Maddy said softly. "Are you okay?"

"No."

"Me neither. Take me home before I get really pissed."

"Wait a minute, why are you angry? It wasn't *my* fault!"

"Well, it wasn't *mine.*"

"But—how could—I don't think . . . ."

"Just get me home, Max," she said, and squeezed his shoulder. "Before something else bad happens."

Detention One

SUGGESTED MUSICOGRAPHY

Jerry Lee Lewis—"Baby Bye Bye"

Dr. Dre and Tupac—"California Love"

The Juliana Hatfield Three—"My Sister"

Max kicked off his wet Chuck Taylors, hung his coat on the rack by the door, and shook the snowflakes from his hair. Maddy and he stood in the dining room, soaking the russet colored shag with melting snow.

"Mom's going to be pissed when she sees this," Maddy pointed at the growing dark splotches beneath their feet.

Max shrugged.

Maddy shrugged in return. "They should've let school out early. A snowstorm on the first of November—only in fucking Iowa," she grumbled.

It was odd, Max thought, but she grumbled like a troll. "They should've *canceled* school," he said, and was going to tell her about the weather report he saw last night, but the sound of Melissa crying stopped him.

"Jesus. What's wrong with her *now*?" Max asked, rubbing his forehead.

Melissa, who had been firmly placed between Max and Maddy in birth, was around the corner and down the hall in her bedroom, sobbing again. She always had something to cry about, at least since she became involved with Jack back in middle school. For quite some time, her tears had done nothing but annoy Max. He still smarted from all the malicious schemes Melissa had plotted against him, simply because he wasn't as "cool" as her boyfriend. Like when she brought one of Jack's friends over and let him rifle through all of Max's comics when he wasn't home. This was something Max would never forget or forgive.

She would have let that asshole take some, too, if Dad hadn't come home from work early that day and found them in my *room, going through* my *stuff.* Max made a fist with his good hand. *Fuck her.*

Maddy turned from him and yelled down the darkened blue hallway. "Mom, Dad," she asked, "what's wrong with Mel?"

"It's not what you think," Dad said from the opposite direction. He was in the kitchen. His voice sounded unusually defeated. "It's not Jack."

Max and Maddy's eyes met.

"The baby, then?" Max mouthed.

They crept toward the sound of Dad's voice as their father appeared in the dining room.

"It's me. I have leukemia." Dad was never one to beat around the bush. "That's why your sister is crying."

"Leukemia?" Max echoed.

"Yep, I won't be around for the end of the world." Dad's voice cracked as he spoke, but his voice wasn't one to crack—ever. It was unnatural and unnerving.

"Y2K is crap, Dad," Max replied, locking his eyes on the gray walls of the dining room and old family photos, the ones where he had a bright blond mullet, thick framed glasses he didn't need anymore, and a goofy smile.

"This isn't funny," Maddy said.

Dad nodded. "I have it pretty bad."

"How bad is 'pretty bad?'" Maddy leaned into the dining room table. Her gesture shook the vase of dead roses, spilling brackish water on the varnish. The roses were from Mom's birthday in September. They had been beyond saving for several weeks, but Dad continued to water them daily.

"It's why I've been so sick lately." Dad walked back to the kitchen, rested against the counter, and studied the intricate designs on the brown tiles at his feet, as if there was a hidden message in the angular shapes. His hair hung over his shoulders in sad black and gray mottles. "It's why I've been to the doctor so much."

Maddy followed him and wrapped her arms around his waist, "Dad?" she asked, "How bad? I mean, you said—"

"It can't be *that* bad," Max interrupted, following Maddy into the kitchen.

Dad sighed and put one hand on Maddy's shoulder, "I don't want to lie to you," he looked at Max, "to any of you." He closed his eyes and took a deep breath. Outside the wind grew angrier.

"He's got the worst kind there is, and they think it's pretty far along," Mom said, entering the kitchen from the hall and standing beside Max. She had been in Melissa's room. The sobs, though dulled, trailed her like ghosts.

Mom was wearing one of Dad's old Ramones t-shirts. Max could see the wet spots where Melissa's tear drops and snot had stained it. Mom's eyes were bloodshot and her cheeks were tinted red. She looked at Dad. "I can't be in there with her anymore. She won't stop cryin' and all she talks about is how she wishes Jack was here—as if that would help."

"Babe . . . " Dad intervened, "not now."

"The worst kind?" Max asked. He noticed Mom was using her normally buried Missouri accent. *Is that whiskey on her breath, too?* "What does that even mean?"

Moses, who must have been trapped in Melissa's bedroom with Mom, ran up to Max and shoved her head under his hand. One of Max's chores was to walk her everyday after school—rain, snow, or shine. She was wagging her stubby tail and dancing around his legs.

Max gently batted her away, "No, not now. In a little bit."

"It means I'm running out of options, Max," Dad said as his son struggled with the dog. "I have Acute Myeloid Leukemia. You don't want to know the details." Dad attempted a chuckle but it was more of a feeble sigh.

"Don't laugh," Maddy whimpered, still clinging to her father.

Dad closed his eyes. "At four, your mom and I are going to see a specialist who's got all the latest test results. We'll know more after that."

Maddy's face was shoved into Dad's chest. "You're not going to die, are you, Daddy?" Her words were muffed. She looked up into his dark eyes. Tears streaked her cheeks and Dad's blue, tie-dyed t-shirt was damp where her face had been buried.

Dad patted Maddy's back and gently pushed her away, saying, "I have to go talk to Melissa. She's taking this news pretty hard. I need to calm her down before she goes into labor."

"Shouldn't Jack be here comforting her, or is he not her boyfriend today?" Max asked, his lips shaking from the bad taste that name put in his mouth.

The house fell as quiet as a morgue.

Dad gave Max a quick, cold glare. "Don't Maxwell. Not now."

What the fuck? Max bit the inside of his cheek. *Mom's allowed to talk shit, but I'm not? Maybe I should tell them about the fight after all.* When he caught Moses staring at him, Max was sure it was disgust he saw in her eyes, or wonder at his comment. It almost seemed like she thought he was stupid. *You've got to be kidding me.* Max lifted his hands, palms out, and backed away from his family. "So, um . . . did you guys just find out, then?"

"About an hour or so ago," Mom said, "I didn't make any supper."

Mom usually started supper around mid-afternoon, shortly after getting home from work. She stayed in her brown and yellow Ducky Burger uniform and let whatever she was making simmer, boil, stew, or bake. When supper was all done, she would turn off the oven and take a shower, eliminating the smell of food from her clothes for the entire night. But Mom wasn't in her uniform this afternoon. Then Max realized the familiar aroma of something—anything—cooking in the kitchen was absent. It made the house feel dead.

"Sorry," Mom stood next to Max and opened the refrigerator. "Do y'all want me to make you somethin?'"

"No," Maddy answered.

"I just need a pop," Max said.

"Well, you guys stay in here." Dad studied them for an uncomfortably long time. As he walked away, the sound of his footsteps tapering down the hall reminded Max of a horror movie. He couldn't remember which one, or if the tapering footsteps were from the victim or the ax-wielding lunatic, but he knew it was creepy.

In an uncharacteristic move, Moses didn't follow Dad, but remained in the kitchen. She was still eyeing Max.

Contempt, Max thought. *That's what she's staring at me with. Contempt. That's fucked up.* He looked at Mom. "How long has Mel been crying?"

"She been cryin' like that for about eight months now, Max. Y'all know that." Mom began rummaging through the refrigerator. "At least today it's been about her father's cancer and not whatever damn fool thing Jack has done, is doin,' or will do. I swear, what else can happen this year?" Standing at the open refrigerator door, she listed off events on her fingers, "Mel gets pregnant, drops out. You break your damn arm playin' flag football—in gym class of all things." She frowned at Max. "I don't think you're ever going to be out of that cast. And you," she pointed at Maddy, "your counselor's a toucher!"

"They say bad things happen in threes. So, it should be over for us, right?" Max offered.

"That's four bad things," Maddy corrected, opening the oak cupboards Dad had cut, drilled, built, and sanded himself five summers earlier. She took out a box of cheese flavored sandwich crackers. "At least Mr. Mickey never touched me."

Mr. Mickey was a dirty old man who became a counselor so he could convince young, unstable women that touching, kissing, and all sorts of other sordid activities were necessary in his office. Max remembered when authorities had to drag the counselor off the school campus in handcuffs before the final bell rang on an August Friday. Though Maddy claimed Mr. Mickey never touched her, sexually or otherwise, Mom still held some contention.

Why would she even bring that up? Max thought.

Mom placed a can of Mtn. Dew in Max's hands. "Come sit down with me for awhile." She looked at Maddy. "You too."

They followed their mother without argument, and took their seats at the small round table in the kitchen. But the seats they went to when they gathered around the table as a family, even after seven years, now seemed foreign.

Everything looks the same though, Max thought. The walls were still a calming shade of light blue. Knick-knacks lining the handmade, inlaid, wooden shelves continued to smile with big, ignorant grins. The gaudy cuckoo clock above the sliding-glass door was still gaudy.

Max could hear the steady, dull hum of the heater in the basement and knew it was filling the house with warmth, but couldn't feel it. He stared at the sweat on his soda can and popped the tab open. Then he followed Mom's gaze through the sliding-glass door to the old oak in the backyard.

Maddy opened her box of sandwich crackers and began stacking them in the middle of the table.

Max took his eyes away from the tree. "That looks like an obelisk."

"What does?" Maddy asked.

"Your cracker stack."

"What's an obelisk?"

"Like the Tower of Babel."[15]

"I don't know what that is either."

"In the Bible, some guys built a—"

Maddy looked up with a frown. "I don't care," she said, cutting him off, "and I might be wrong, but I don't think that was an 'obelisk.'"

"Y'all know," Mom interrupted, "my old dog, Champ, died of cancer. So did my mama, your grandma."

"We know," Maddy said.

"Dad's going to be okay, Mom," Max added.

"He's tough."

"He is; you're right," Mom agreed, "but cancer's pretty damn tough too."

"But it's practically the year 2000, they've got to be able to fix him," Max hoped, "right?"

"That's what they're sayin,' yeah, but I don't know. Your dad hadn't had a physical in almost a year when they caught it, and . . . all those damn tests and procedures to tell us . . . ." Mom kept her eyes on the tree swaying in the backyard, hunched under the snow and ice. "It snows too damn much in Iowa." She reached across the table and took out a handful of crackers from Maddy's box.

Max stood, fed up with the smell of salty sandwich crackers caked with fake cheese. *When the hell did these "tests and procedures" happen?*

---

[15] In The Bible, "Book of Genesis," there is this story about a tower people build so they could reach heaven. Outraged, God made it so they all spoke different languages because He didn't want them to reach the heavens. Religion is weird.

He wondered. "I'm going to take Moses for a walk before I go to work." Max put his hand in his side pocket and felt the tightly rolled joint Paul had given him.

"Max, you don't have to today."

"No, I want to."

"Just try and be back before we leave," Mom said. She stood up and Maddy followed.

"You want to come, Maddy?" Max asked, giving his sister a knowing glance.

She weighed the idea for a moment, and then said, "No, I want to see Mel when Dad's done."

Max shrugged. As if on cue, Dad reappeared in the kitchen. He leaned his hand on the yellow vinyl countertop. He smiled at his daughter again and took his wife's hand as she passed him. The women went on down the hall toward Melissa's bedroom. Max turned away from his father.

Moses whined.

"How're you feeling, Max?" Dad asked when Mom and Maddy were out of earshot.

"You read that in a parenting book?" Max replied, laughing as he looked out the sliding-glass doors; the snow, manic ballerinas, whirled and twirled in the cold air. The wind was still whirling, but it slowed some. It gave the scene an eerie, serene feel, like a Grant Wood painting.[16]

He contemplated not going for a walk, despite the drama and the joint in his pocket aching to be smoked. Dad stared at him with a small, quivering smile hiding behind his beard.

Is he ashamed? Max wondered, noticing the lack of a return quip to his parenting book jab.

Dad raised an eyebrow, and moved his head from side to side in a deliberate manner that Max had come to regard as pleasant disdain. "Maxwell, be serious for a second. How are you taking this?"

---

[16] *American Gothic* isn't the only thing Grant Wood is known for, it is his *starkness* that tends to captivate his fans. Not as cool as your standard comic book artist, but you know, his work has its time and place.

Max offered his father a loud, fake laugh before mimicking his movements. "Well, other than the fact I just found out my dad could be dead this time next year, yeah, I'm okay," he retorted. "Happy Halloween! Oh, and here's a snowstorm!" Then he clapped to top off his performance.

Dad didn't reply.

"What do you want me to say?" Max asked, the tension building in his body, creeping out through his voice.

"Don't talk to your father like that," Mom's voice cracked like a whip as she reappeared in the kitchen.

Max recalled her ability to just *know,* at all times, what was going on in every room in her house. *She's freaking Marvel Girl.*[17]

"Max—"

"No," Dad stood. "Let him take Moses for a walk. She needs one, and the way this snow is falling, they won't be going later."

***

Max dug his warmest winter wear out of the hall closet, including an oversized brown parka that would fit over his cast, and walked out the door with Moses in tow. The snow was drifting higher. There was no more sleet, just a steady deluge of snow. He put his head down against the biting wind and tried not to think about any of it. Moses pranced around him like a reindeer.

There was a small patch of desolate trees a few blocks from the Dinkman home, far enough from any streets or houses that Max felt comfortable letting Moses run free when they went there. He also felt the area was private enough to spark up a joint in the middle of the afternoon — especially during a snowstorm.

Even with heavy snow falling from the gray sky, the smell of death permeated the woods. He walked on inches of fallen brown leaves covered by a deceitful white blanket. Trees were like aged sentries, guarding

---

[17] Jean Grey, the original mutant female, known as Marvel Girl before she took the moniker "The Phoenix," has the power to read minds, levitate objects, and be an all around ass kicking ass kicker for the ironically named X-Men.

something long forgotten that nobody cared about. The normally dried up creek running through the center of the small forest, damp due to the new snow, seemed sad and alone.

Max brushed off a rotted log in the clearing and freed Moses from her leash. She dashed, chasing some winter rodent Max couldn't see. He watched the snow kick up behind her feet and followed her barks as the sounds trailed off on their own adventure. When she was out of sight, he hefted his collar up around his face. He took off his left glove, pulled the joint and a blue Bic lighter from his pocket, placed the paper against his lips, and lit it on his first try.

"Tiny victories," he told himself with a sad smile.

Max breathed in heavily; the familiar smell of freshly cut grass invaded his nostrils. Tendrils of smoke spun like effervescent batons. He regarded the forest, ignored the icy weather, and let the weed work its magic. His eyes became tired and dry. Max thought he heard Moses scratching at a tree trunk somewhere.

"Nice," he said, taking another hit, "this is nice." *It'd be even better if I were on a sunny beach in California.* Dr. Dre and Tupac[18] started rapping in his mind. He bobbed his head, softly singing the only words he knew, *"California lo-ove . . . . Shake it, shake it baby, shake it, shake it mama . . . ."*

After Max repeated the same lines several times, Moses came back, sat down in the snow across from him, and stared. Max found himself staring back. Her eyes were black holes.

"Hey," he said between drags, "I know why you never liked Laura. The bitch was a liar."

Moses cocked her head to the side, but kept on staring.

He reached over and petted her wet head, trying to get her to look away. She wouldn't. It was starting to bug him.

---

[18] Two pioneers of rap in the 90s who managed to bring the world of hip hop to Midwestern white boys like Max. Ironically, Eazy-E (another gangsta rapper) was quite vocal in his accusations that Dr. Dre was gay in his song "Real Muthaphuckkin G's."

"What the hell, Mos? Why didn't you tell me about her?" He waited for a response he knew he wouldn't get. He shivered. "Whatever."

Max closed his eyes and imagined he was Wolverine.[19] Nothing could stop him. *Once, Magneto ripped out all the adamantium from Wolverine's bones and he nearly died. God, he's so hardcore. He's probably been stabbed, shot, beaten, and tortured more than any other superhero.[20]* Max tapped his shoes against the ground. *Wolverine's never had cancer though. Captain Marvel died of cancer.[21] He'll probably come back to life someday.*

One of the reasons Max loved comic books was because death wasn't permanent. A good resurrection story could conquer death, and Max saw nothing wrong with that. Several fans hated that death was so impermanent in comics. To them, it was a form of artistic self-belittling, but to Max, it was beautiful.

Bucky[22] would probably come back to life some day. Uncle Ben[23] too. Batman's parents[24] maybe. Cancer, he thought. *Fucking cancer.*

Max remembered having bologna sandwiches and water for supper as a little boy, and when an open oven heated their trailer in the wintertime. He remembered his parents having to choose between Christmas and medicine for Maddy when she had spinal meningitis as a

---

[19] Wolverine, AKA Patch, AKA Logan. Coolest mutant hero ever—Wolverine was born with a healing factor, claws, and a skeletal structure that was later laced with the strongest metal in the Marvel Universe—adamantium.

[20] All of these events have happened throughout various issues of *X-Men, Uncanny X-Men, Wolverine,* and other comics, but the most significant would be the adamantium being ripped from his bones—issue #25 of *X-Men.*

[21] Captain Mar-Vell was a Kree (galaxy sprawling alien civilization) soldier sent to earth to infiltrate the planet's society. But he fell in love with mankind and became one of the greatest heroes the world had ever known. He fought off everything from alien invasions to manmade monsters in his career, only to die at the hands of cancer. His story is quite possibly Marvel Comics' finest hour.

[22] Bucky Barnes, a spunky little soldier who sacrificed his life to stop evil Nazi bastards. He was Captain America's first sidekick.

[23] Uncle Ben gave Peter Parker the most important lesson of his life before getting gunned down by a burglar—"With great power comes great responsibility."

[24] When Bruce Wayne was a child, his parents were brutally murdered on the streets of Gotham City before their impressionable son's young eyes. These above named characters are some of the perennially *dead* characters in popular comics . . . or are they . . . ?

baby. He remembered feeling a red-hot anger that Santa would take his Christmas away because Maddy was sick and thinking how unfair it was. But he also remembered being happy that Maddy came home from the hospital alive, and not dead, though he didn't really know what that meant at the time.

As all the memories piled up, Max realized they equaled one thing: victory. His family had "overcome hardships." It sounded like something out of bad book, but it was true. Now, on the verge of Max, Maddy, and Melissa's leap into the real world, Melissa got pregnant and Dad got leukemia.

It isn't fair. Max knew he wasn't an angel. If his parents discovered how much weed he smoked, they would probably make him live with Dad's weird second cousin in Middle-of-Nowhere, Nebraska, or worse—make him live with Mom's Dad, wherever that was. *Oh, and what else? Laura "found out" I was gay! Fuck her.*

Max didn't have a problem with homosexuals. His parents had instilled in him a healthy liberalism that was oftentimes troublesome; living in what Max considered one of the least tolerant towns in one of the least tolerant counties in one of the least tolerant states in one of the least tolerant countries in the world. He had even contemplated homosexuality a few times for no other reason than to piss off the powers that be. Max didn't know who the powers that be were, but he had always thought coming out of the closet would be a great way to piss them off.

I could be Northstar,[25] he thought. *I know I got issue 106*[26] *somewhere . . . I could read it again and get some pointers . . . . Seems like a lot of trouble though . . . and Wolverine is so much cooler.* Max sheathed his six imaginary adamantium claws and opened his eyes. "Well shit." The joint dwindled to barely a roach in his shivering hand. He was high. His body tingled. *Maybe*

---

[25] Northstar, Jean-Paul Baubier, another mutant hero, super fast and super gay (he really is a homosexual, that's not derogatory). Not that it is important, but he is Canadian . . . and so is Wolverine. Incidentally, both have been in the superhero group, Alpha Flight, at one time or another.

[26] This, of course, is the most famous issue of *Alpha Flight* in which Northstar reveals his sexuality to the world.

I'm just cold. The snow had covered his tracks like a predator trying to confuse him. *How long have I been out here? And why is that fucking dog still staring at me?* "It's late. We better go." He put out the joint and placed it in his coat pocket carefully, as if it was the bone marrow sample his old science teacher said leukemia patients needed to survive.

He placed Moses' leash back on and headed home. Although the growing mounds of snow were getting harder to maneuver through, Max felt like he was floating. The cold was beginning to bother him—it even smelled chilly. But he didn't notice the houses covered in frost, the scraping sounds of men shoveling, or the cars creeping down the street for fear of a slippery spot. Max's world was veiled in a hazy white film, like a television with a bad signal. His mind knew he had to be home and his body knew how to get there, so he walked. Everything else slipped to the back of his brain.

When he was a short distance from his house, he saw Mom and Dad edge by in their gray Saturn sedan. Max wondered how long it had been since the whole family was together in that car. He waved at them. Dad leaned over and gave him a thumbs-up from the driver's side. Max couldn't help but think there was some form of irony being presented in that gesture.

Moses tried to race for the porch, but Max's slow pace held her back.

Maddy opened the door and grimaced at him as she slid her coat over her shoulders. "Shop More called," she hollered, her eyes teary and red. "You don't have to work tonight."

Max nodded, but didn't know if she noticed.

"It's really starting to come down out there." Maddy wrapped her coat further around her body. "I bet they'll cancel school tomorrow."

***

Max and Maddy sat at the kitchen table, which was still covered in empty Chinese take-out boxes left over from dinner. Even though they had eaten hours ago, they couldn't get up. Dad and Mom had gone to bed early and Melissa shortly after, leaving Max and Maddy to themselves and their thoughts.

Max nudged his Mtn. Dew can with his finger. His mind digested how his parents had said very little about Dad's doctor visit, and exuded a false happiness that was both nauseating and frightening. He turned his attention to the clock—it read 11:33pm.

Outside, an eerie whistle blew drifts of snow against the garage.

Maddy shuddered. "I can't believe it stopped snowing," she sighed, disappointed. "Now they definitely won't cancel school tomorrow."

"More good news," Max grumbled and leaned his head back, rubbing his eyes.

Moses walked into the kitchen then, sniffing the air. The house, silent except for Max and Maddy's half-hearted attempts at conversation, sounded with the echoes of the dog's claws clicking across the tile.

"Hey Moses," Maddy tried to smile. She turned away from the dying blizzard outside to pet the dog's head.

"She probably has to go out," Max sighed.

"Probably," Maddy agreed. She gathered the take-out boxes into her arms and tried to clean up. After dumping the food remains into the trash, she leaned against the counter, watching Moses sit at Max's feet.

"You want to go out?" Max asked.

Moses looked up at him with her large, dark eyes, unaffected by his words.

"*Outside?*" Max clarified, hoping to get some kind of reaction other than her odd look.

Moses only continued staring.

"What's her problem?" Maddy wondered aloud. "She's just, like, staring at you. Why's she doing that?"

"How should I know?"

"It's creepy."

"You're telling me."

Maddy washed her hands and walked around Moses to sit back down. She crossed her arms on the table and laid her head on them, watching

Moses watch Max. After a few minutes, she closed her eyes and asked, "Do you think Dad's really going to die?"

"All they need is one bone marrow match. They've got to be able to find that, right?"

"No," Melissa's voice sounded like a judge's hammer in the dark, "they won't."

Max and Maddy glanced up, surprised, while Moses offered a small growl of disapproval.

"Shut up," Melissa snapped. She intended to silence Moses with an intense glare, but the dog consummately ignored her.

"What? Why?" Max asked, confused.

"Because," Melissa said, taking her spot at the table between her older brother and younger sister, "everyone the insurance company will pay for has already been tested. No one matched."

"That doesn't make sense," Maddy said, her voice strained. "I thought they only found out a couple weeks ago."

"Yeah," Max added. "Shut up, Mel. You don't know what you're talking about."

Melissa grunted, momentarily gazing at the bare kitchen table like a hungry cow in a barren field. "Hey, did you guys throw away the leftovers?"

"Who cares," Max ground out through gritted teeth. "What do you know that we don't?"

"A lot, apparently," she sighed before patting her gigantic belly.

Rage toward Melissa's smug, flippant attitude was forcing itself out. But before Max could think of something to say, Maddy spoke.

"Just fucking tell us, Melissa!" she almost shouted, her voice dancing near the border of madness.

Melissa glanced at Maddy, almost affectionately. "Look, they've known about Dad's cancer for a while. Like, months. They've been waiting for a match to tell you, but they could only get three tests, and none of them matched. If Dad was going to be okay, you two still wouldn't know anything about this."

"We haven't been tested," Max argued. "Can't they search for more?"

"Why wouldn't they tell us?" Maddy almost whimpered, locking gazes with her sister.

"No," Melissa continued. "Maddy doesn't match—they already had a sample from when she was really sick. Remember? And Max, they had a sample from when you broke your arm. We have too much Mom in us."

"Whatever," Max said. "Why would they tell you and not us?"

Tears rolled down Maddy's cheeks. Max reached his hand across the table for her to hold. She gripped his fingers.

"They didn't *tell me* anything," Melissa said, as though this fact should have been obvious. "I'm here all the time. I *knew* something was wrong. I *knew* all those trips to the doctor weren't normal for Dad. I *knew*." She pushed away from the table and stood, looking down on her siblings with the contempt of an irritated queen. "You guys think I've been crying because of this," she pointed at her stomach, "but you're wrong. This is the only happy thing in my life right now. It's going to bring Jack and me closer together."

Max rolled his eyes.

Melissa narrowed hers. "Dad's going to die, guys. All that shit they said when they got back from the doctor is a lie." She walked away, ignoring Max's snide, exasperated sighs, and turned to face them one last time. "You know that hollow feeling you have right now? Get used to it. Oh, and Mom's been spending a lot of time on the phone with Dad's insurance, so if she smells like whiskey, that's why." She waited until the information sank into her siblings' brains before jerking her head away, and departed for her bedroom.

Max and Maddy exchanged broken looks.

"Mom and Dad lied to us?" she whispered.

"I hate Mel," Max said, avoiding her question. "Don't listen to her, Mad. Everything'll be fine."

Maddy nodded, but she was still crying.

Max grimaced. Then he got an idea, something to distract Maddy, and hopefully, himself, from their dad's cancer. "Hey," he asked before he could stop himself, "what's Taylor's phone number?"

Lesson Two: Sex Education

Tuesday November 2, 1999

At 6:30am, before daylight broke, Max woke up. Outside, the rising temperature was turning the ice and snow into watery brown slush. Inside, Mom and Dad were already awake and active. While Dad filled out the paperwork for his leave of absence, Mom, on the phone in what Max thought was a sadly subdued voice, attempted to explain Dad's situation to her boss and beg for a few more days off this year. Melissa was watching television and eating a bowl of cereal in bed. Max yawned and hoped she would drop the bowl. Maddy slept.

Max decided to call Taylor as soon as the smiling weatherman announced school was still in session. He knew if he thought about it for too long he would change his mind, and he didn't want that. Max was relatively certain Maddy called Taylor the night before to tell her he had asked for her phone number.

She probably knows I'm going to call.

When Mom hung up the phone and walked away, grinding her teeth, Max opted not to ask her about the phone call and made his instead. He dialed slowly; there was a quiet part of him saying this was a bad idea. Taylor wasn't exactly the type of girl a sane man would want to lose his virginity to, but Max was desperate. If the rumors floating around school were true, Taylor had a working knowledge of sex and knew how to make a man happy. He could use that sort of female lover.

It'll be fine. I'll just . . . be sure to use a condom. Yeah.

The phone rang.

Max knew their hook up would be Taylor's dream come true, since Maddy had told him so—on several occasions. He wasn't sure why he didn't like her the way she liked him. She was a hot little Irish girl with stereotypical thick flaming curls many men had spent many nights trying to get wrapped up in. On top of that, she was kind to small animals, quick witted, and intelligent. Despite her promiscuity, she was out of Max's league. He knew if they ever got together, she would be the one dating down.

God, I can't do this. I don't even like *her,* Max thought. *Shit, maybe Laura is right, maybe I am gay.*

The phone rang again.

All this time he thought he was just comfortable with his sexuality. *But if I were gay, would it really be such a big deal?* Max stared at the ceiling. *If Laura would've taken my virginity, maybe I would know for sure . . . .*

One more ring.

His hand reached for Laura's letter, still safely tucked into his back pocket. Her claim was convincing. After all, she did know him better than anyone. Though she had essentially ditched him when she went off to college, the way Mom had said she would, Max still trusted her. Sure, he was still pissed at her, so much so he couldn't imagine ever seeing her again and not punching her in the gut, or face, or both.

Hell, now that she came out of the closet, isn't hitting her just like hitting a dude? Max's shoulders slumped. *No . . . . She wouldn't have written something like this just to mess with my head . . . would she?* He didn't want to think so.

Four rings.

Max was about to hang up, then he heard Taylor's soft, expectant voice.

"Hello?"

He cringed against the phone. Taylor annoyed him. Max thought she was too nice, like her lovable behavior was fake, but it wasn't, which made Max feel worse.

I bet this is why she's had so many partners, he told himself. *I can't do this. I can't.*

But he did.

"Taylor? This is Max. Do you need a ride to school?"

"Sure," she said, her tone dripping with zeal.

Max hung up the phone and woke Maddy. He lied to her about his intentions with Taylor, and convinced her to get a ride to school with Paul's mom. He felt like a douche bag. Taylor was Maddy's best friend, and Maddy was Max's. Best friends didn't lie or keep secrets from each other, and he was doing both.

She'll understand later, he hoped, momentarily shunting to the outskirts of his mind all the information he possessed about Maddy's disposition. As he walked out the front door, started his car, scraped the frost, and drove slowly down the street, Max couldn't shake the thought that this was not going to end well.

* * *

Around school, it was common knowledge that Taylor knew more about the male body than most men. On the drive to her house, Max shook his unease by asking himself the rhetorical question: *What's one more name on her list?* Taylor actually liked him too. He wouldn't be one of her conquests. To her, this would be the start of a relationship she had always wanted.

Max grimaced, glancing in his rearview mirror and ignoring the eerie way the face reflecting back at him looked like Mom. *I'm so going to hell.*

When he pulled up to Taylor's house and honked the horn, he saw her face light up as she peeked out the beige living room curtains. When she got in the car, Max noticed her smile, her smell—everything about her was inviting, sweet, and naïve. The douche bag feeling came back.

He tried to grin. "Do you want to skip?"

She nodded, not even asking about Maddy.

Max drove to Vander Veer Park in the middle of town. It was a vast, tree filled stretch of land between two perpetually busy one-way roads. On one end was a giant white fountain made out of stone Max couldn't name. Speckled up and down the park were various playgrounds and regions of grass-covered fields. On the other end, by the parking lot, was a shallow pond. In a couple months, there would be hordes of kids in fluffy pink and blue hats and coats skating over the ice. They would all be chattering smiles, ignorant and happy with childhood.

And stupid, Max thought.

On November 2nd though, the pond was still, cold, and depressing. Melting snow turned most of the surrounding area into black mud and now, two hours since Max had crawled out of bed, the sun decided to hide away again, giving everything in the park a tint of gray. Max wondered if Taylor, standing next to him with her hands in her coat pockets, could picture the same thing he could—all the carefree kids and their wintertime merriment. He could feel the excited tension ooze from her, and knew the fictional scene was making her happy.

I really suck, he thought.

An eerie, unsure silence hung over them as they stared at the muddy, only partially iced-over pond.

"So what's up?" she finally asked.

Maddy should've at least told her about Dad, Max pondered. He was certain Maddy was telling everyone in her first period class about Dad, even though the night before their parents had said, over a nonchalant dinner of Chinese take-out, to keep it quiet for a while. Maddy probably told Taylor about Laura officially dumping him, too. What he didn't know was whether Maddy told Taylor Laura was gay.

He forced a yawn and rubbed his eyes. "You know about my dad, right?"

Taylor nodded with tears in her eyes. Her dad was the definition of "deadbeat," and she looked to Max's father as a replacement. Taylor loved him. Max knew her tears were genuine, not show. The douche bag feeling hit him again, hard.

"He isn't going to die, Max," she said, not convincing either of them.

"I don't know." Max shrugged. "Mel said he's had it for a while . . ." his voice broke, "and they were keeping it from us."

"What does Mel know?"

He shrugged again. "Not much . . . but I don't know . . . it makes sense . . . ."

Taylor wrapped her arms around his waist and placed her head on his chest. "How are you, Maxwell?"

Max felt her hair tickle the bottom of his chin as his chest rose with a deep breath. "I'm okay," he lied. Every cell in his body was lighting up. *Revulsion?* he considered, *Or arousal?*

"Then why are we skipping class to stare at a pond in the cold?"

"I don't know. I didn't feel like going to school today."

She was quiet again.

Max sighed.

Taylor's fingers gently dug into his coat as she squeezed him. "I know why you called me," she said. "Maddy told me about Laura too."

"Everything?" Max asked. He tried to move back a step, and reached for the letter still tucked in his back pocket.

Taylor clung to him. "She dumped you."

"Anything else?"

"What else is there?"

"Nothing," Max said through a sigh.

"I'm willing to be your rebound girl, Max," she said after a lengthy silence, "because I love you."

This is fucking ridiculous. He hated to hear her say that. Her words seemed sad, juvenile, and wrong. She might have been infatuated with him—how that happened was beyond his scope of knowledge—but he knew she didn't really love him, and he didn't love her.

I have to try . . . maybe I can learn to like her?

Max lifted his broken arm up and around her shoulder, resting it on the nape of her neck. His guilt for what he wanted to do with her grew in his belly like a demon baby. She was a good person. He felt sorry for her. Taylor had a rough life, an alcoholic mom, loser dad, and a couple of little sisters that needed her attention to survive. Max's conscience started scolding him, telling him Taylor didn't deserve the treachery he was planning. Sweat trailed down the sides of his face.

Is this treachery though? he wondered. *I mean, she has wanted this for a long time, hasn't she? Oh God, what the fuck am I doing? Can I really do this?*

In some respects, Taylor was more of a sister to Maddy than Melissa was. They talked about everything together, and were often considered inseparable. Even Mom had developed a tight kinship with her. She had been plotting with Maddy to hook him up with Taylor for years. If they found out he was using Taylor for sex, Max didn't know if he could handle their disappointment.

Then again, he thought, *Mom did betray me when she kept Dad's illness a secret, so why should I care? And Maddy's always trying to get me to hang out with Taylor . . . . So she should be happy, right?* Max looked up into the gray sky. He wanted solid proof he wasn't gay—something to shove in Laura's face the next time he saw her. *That will make me feel better about everything.*

A battle akin to *Secret Wars* brewed inside him. Max's psyche became Battleworld, and The Beyonder had taken many of the heroes and villains of his comic book riddled youth and placed them there so they could battle for his morality. It was massive. Some died. Some were reborn. Classic costumes changed. But in the end, there was no cosmic difference, there was no lasting effect.[27]

Thinking back to his burgeoning years as a comic book fan, Max could remember feeling slightly cheated by the storyline, as though there was a lot of hype for something that ended up being far less important than it was advertised to be.

Taylor lifted up her head and looked into Max's eyes. He thought she wanted him to lose himself in her green plates, but he couldn't.

To hide his indifference, he leaned down to place a rushed kiss on her lips.

Surprisingly, Max kind of enjoyed it. She tasted different than Laura. There was no harsh cigarette overtone clouding everything. Her lips were just sweet, like grape soda. Max accepted the fact that all kisses affected him, even bad ones. On some basic level, he associated them with pizza, a bad slice was better than no slice. But a kiss wasn't satisfying enough—he needed more.

Taylor pulled away and took his hands in hers.

---

[27] Okay, so nobody died, but it was a big deal in 1984 that changed nothing important. The Beyonder took a bunch of Marvel heroes and villains to a different planet and told them to fight. How cool is that? Spider-Man got his black costume, and new characters emerged like the second Spider-Woman, Titania, and the wholly forgettable Volcana.

"Let's go back to my house," she cooed, "no one's home."

I always felt something when Laura kissed me, Max speculated while he held Taylor's hands tightly, noticing their warmth. *But if I'm gay, I wouldn't have felt anything with Laura, right? What if I don't feel anything with Taylor, even after . . . sex?*

Taylor was determined to prove to Max she would make an excellent rebound girl. She was talking to him, softly again, a seductive yet warped mix of shame and desire—but Max wasn't listening. His thoughts continued to wander. He remembered the song "Scarecrow[28]" by Melissa Etheridge that Ms. Deftly had played to his class a few weeks ago. An image of Matthew Sheppard hanging on a fence in Laramie, Wyoming flashed across his mind.

But Davenport, Iowa isn't exactly Laramie, Wyoming, is it? Then he remembered Brandon Teena, the transgendered teen in Nebraska the movie, *Boys Don't Cry,*[29] was based on. He shivered. Iowa wasn't that far away from Nebraska.

Taylor suddenly pressed against him, as if trying to recapture his attention. He felt her breasts, her nipples hard from the cold, shove into him through their clothes. *That* he liked.

Problem solved.

"Well?" Taylor asked.

Max shoved his conscious into the deepest corner of his mind, "Okay."

***

Taylor's house looked like a nice, normal Midwestern suburban home. It was an odd shade of green, but well painted. The driveway was smooth, the yard was manicured, and there wasn't a hint of trashiness about it. But Max had been there a few times before to pick up Maddy. He knew the outside was just a mask.

---

[28] "Scarecrow," a song by Melissa Etheridge, is a tribute to Matthew Sheppard, a boy who was killed because of his sexuality.
[29] Brandon Teena, born a female, preferred life in a male identity until some bigots discovered his secret, raped, and then murdered him.

When they opened the side door, Max felt bile bubble up in the back of his throat once the smell hit him—it was a mixture of pee-soaked sheets, liquor puke, and dirt. He swooned.

How does Maddy come over here all the time?

The kitchen, where they entered, was covered in waste that had manifested its own consciousness and sectioned itself off into neat layers. Wet garbage sat like a king on a throne beneath the window, gray light from the overcast sky falling on it like ash. Used diapers knelt next to the garbage, putrid facsimiles of courtiers. The table held a colony of dirty dishes. Piles of old newspapers, crinkled and yellowing, leaned against the counter, like lazy guards. The recycling bin was spilling over and into the small closet that was, at one time, a pantry, but had now become some sort of storage space for items deemed recyclable. Pots and pans, crusty with old orange and yellow macaroni and cheese, hardened in the sink. The floor was sticky. A litter box next to the counter, with fresh cat turds, peered up at him.

"Jesus," he said under his breath.

"I know," Taylor turned back, her eyes down and her cheeks flushed with embarrassment. "I don't have a lot of time to clean these days. It's a lot worse than when you were over here last."

"No, no, no," Max shook his head. "I didn't mean . . . it's just . . . wow."

"Come to my room," she said, taking his hand, "it's clean there."

Max let Taylor lead him through the kitchen, weaving around the piles of filth, into the living room. There were toys scattered all over the floor. Some were broken, some intact, and some were partially chewed. A few sad, little dolls stared at him, their drooping eyes vacant. A lone loveseat sat a few feet away from a small television blaring an episode of *Franklin*.[30]

Max hated that little turtle. *What's he bitching about today?* he wondered, and considered giving the television a swift kick to its screen. *I bet you think Mom and Dad will always take care of your stupid problems.* Max thought about his own parents. *Not in the real world, Frankie.*

---

[30] A series of books turned cartoon about a good little turtle boy whose life was just . . . well . . . perfect. I fucking hate him too.

As they walked down the hall, Max dared to touch the walls and noticed they were as sticky as the kitchen floor. Dirty laundry piles as high as his knees lined the walls. He wasn't sure, but he thought he saw one of them move. Max averted his eyes as they passed the bathroom door, but heard the low hum of the vent working. The obstacles were getting to be too much. Max felt like Odysseus.[31] His entire crew dead, so many horrible monstrosities besetting him, he couldn't go on. He didn't care what the gods wanted; all he wanted was to go home. Taylor laughed a little as she opened her bedroom door at the end of the hall. Max changed his mind. Now all he wanted to do was fall to his knees and praise the gods.

Compared to the rest of Taylor's atrocious house, her room was Calypso's island.[32] It wasn't just clean, it was immaculate. The walls were white, the bed was made, her vanity, dresser, and desk were all straightened and orderly. There wasn't a single pair of underwear on the floor. Nothing was out of place. It smelled like the Yankee Candle Store in the mall—warm, clean, and inviting. Max sat on her bed, a fluffy red comforter easing him back to reality.

"Wow," this time there was depth to his voice, amazement, not shock or disgust. "Wow," he said again.

Taylor smiled. "I like to keep my space clean." She took off her coat and stood by her short bookshelf. "You know," she said, "a place where I can be comfortable."

"I see."

"Speaking of that," Taylor glided across the bedroom and sat down next to Max, close enough so their thighs and shoulders touched. "Are you comfortable?" She leaned in and kissed him on his neck. "Why don't you take off your coat?"

---

[31] The main character from Homer's epic poem *The Odyssey,* and one of the first superheroes of the Western world.

[32] Ogygia—Odysseus spent seven years there, alone with Calypso . . . . "Against his will," scholars say. But it took seven years for him to tell her to stop pleasuring him and build a damn boat? Yeah, sounds like a really shitty prison.

Oh God, Max started to squirm. He could hear his old psychology teacher whisper, *When a father and daughter's relationship is strained, the daughter will look for love from males in unhealthy ways.*

Taylor kissed him on the neck again. "Are you sure you're comfortable?"

"Yeah, yeah, yeah, I'm comfortable!" he choked as images of sexually transmitted diseases danced in his head. But her hand on his thigh was electrifying. He imagined one of the drawers on her nightstand was filled with condoms. His palms started to sweat. Max wanted to ask if everything people said about her was true. He twitched a little, his nerves and confusion getting the better of him.

Taylor cocked her head to the side. She looked at him with the same puzzled expression he sometimes got from Moses when he refused to take her for her daily walk.

"What's the matter?"

"I have to go to the bathroom," he blurted out before he could stop himself. *Oh shit!*

"Go ahead," she purred.

Max left her bedroom and found himself walking cautiously through the wilderness of dirty clothes toward the bathroom door hanging half open. He could hear the sound of the vent again, but the light wasn't on. Though it was pathologically clean in Taylor's bedroom, Max suspected the bathroom, being used by two little girls, a teenager, and an alcoholic woman, was not a pretty sight. Max was squeamish when it came to this sort of thing. He neared the door, his feet dragging, and gently shoved it open. He stood for a moment and peered into the darkened room. There were black clumps of what looked like hair on the floor. The shower curtain was closed, but the smell of mildew permeated his olfactory. He turned his head, took a deep breath through his mouth, and flipped on the light.

Max felt faint. There was grit and grime on every surface and a dingy, bleak brown hue to everything he could see. A toothpaste tube sat on the edge of the sink, half of its contents squeezed onto the floor and dripping down the cabinet. The toilet bowl had a yellow tarnish to it that screamed at Max to leave, less he become one with the microscopic creatures living there. And again, this floor was sticky. He wondered if it was pee. Then he wondered how a house full of girls could get pee on the floor. The room was like something out of a bad movie about a country kid who goes to the city to become famous. This was the bathroom that kid would have to use. The kind of bathroom found in a rundown hotel on the wrong side of the tracks, with a crackhead asleep behind the toilet—where people went to die. He gulped and looked in the mirror.

His reflection was speckled with the white dots of dried toothpaste spittle, crusty whitehead remains, and splotches of what appeared to be dried-up hand lotion. His eyes were more inset than normal. Deep purple rings hung below them, and he couldn't keep his mouth shut. There was sweat playing with the idea of forming at his hairline, and his shaggy locks looked limp.

I can't do this, he thought. *I can't.*

"Max?" Taylor's voice called from down the hall. "Is everything okay?"

"Yeah," he replied without thinking. "I'm on my way."

She giggled.

Max's heart pounded. *Why am I so worried? What is bothering me? I want to lose my virginity, don't I? Why can't I do this?* He tried taking a deep breath, but coughed instead. He ran his fingers through his hair and splashed some water on his face. "Okay," he said. "I'm going to do this. Okay . . . okay . . . ."

When Max made it back to Taylor's bedroom, he was not prepared for what he saw.

Taylor was on her bed—naked—her body as freckled and pale as her face. Her breasts were small, pert, and pointed at him like two hot Uncle Sams, each saying, "I want you!"

Max's whole body shook, but he couldn't keep his eyes from absorbing the view. He started at her face, and scanned down. Her belly was flat, but not muscular, soft, but not fat. And in case anyone ever wondered about the authenticity of Taylor's flaming curls . . . .

Max's cheeks were on fire. *The carpet does indeed match the drapes.*

"Do you like what you see?" she asked, her voice so sultry it upped the humidity of the room.

"I . . . ." Max felt woozy. He did like what he saw but this was too much. *I'm not ready. This isn't right.* Despite his instincts screaming Laura was wrong, Max knew this was wrong too. "I'm sorry, Taylor," he murmured. "I thought I could—I want to—but I can't do this."

As Taylor's expression went from seductive to shattered, Max backed out of her room, ran from the house, jumped in his car, and drove to school without looking back.

Lesson Three: Spanish I

SUGGESTED MUSICOGRAPHY

Monty Norman and John Barry—"James

Bond Theme"

Nirvana—"All Apologies"

Enya—"Orinoco Flow"

Peggy Lee—"Fever"

Max pulled into the far end of the parking lot, slid out of his car—being sure to shut the door as quietly as possible—and crept toward the east side of the school. He had to be careful, evasive, like a hero sneaking into an enemy compound. He had to be Daredevil.[33] An all red costume, or perhaps the classic black and yellow—Max didn't care, as far as he was concerned, they were both pretty cool.

He made his stealthy way up the slight grassy incline to one of the many entrances. His heart thudded, he sweat, and the little hairs all over his body stood on end. Silently, he moved closer. Max would have imagined a slick James Bond spy tune[34] to go with his little adventure, but since he was already imagining himself with Daredevil's heightened senses, it would only distract him. He was against the school's brown brick outer-wall, sliding along, looking both ways as he moved.

There was no one around. Max took a few deep breaths to slow the adrenaline, and stepped into a mud puddle, secreted away beneath a heavy coating of wet, dead grass. He fell, slamming onto his back with a SPLAT, knocking the wind out of his lungs, his hat off his head, and his book bag from his hand. He wheezed and flailed around like a dying fish. For a few fleeting moments, Max forgot that he was, in fact, not Daredevil.

Max struggled to his feet. He was sure enough time had passed for someone to notice him but there were no teachers rushing to his aid, no students calling out from the safety of the school. He was alone, wet and muddy. Max hobbled to the nearest entrance, caring little now if anyone saw him, and though he knew all the doors were locked from the inside, he reached for the handle and pulled.

Locked.

---

[33] AKA Matthew Murdock. As a boy, he was hit in the face with a canister of irradiated material, thusly blinded. However, a side effect to his blindness was a super-enhancement of all of his other senses and abilities. He knows when your heart rate increases by a fraction of a second. He knows where you've been all day. He knows if there are any teachers, security guards, or hall monitors about.

[34] The tune is called "James Bond Theme." Monty Norman wrote it and John Barry arranged it. Can you picture that scene from the beginning of every movie? Yeah, that might be more badass than Daredevil. Ian Flemming is the man. He created James Bond.

With any luck, when the bells rang for passing period, the halls would fill with students, and an impressionable freshman would walk by and let him in. Max hugged himself and silently wished he had a watch. When the bell finally did ring, the halls filled, like he knew they would. He didn't stop pounding until a kindhearted freshman boy helped him inside.

***

All day, Max had felt like glue edging down a piece of some kindergartner's construction paper. He swore a cosmic toddler atop a celestial highchair was eyeing him, certain that if he was glue, the particular kindergartner using him was the kind of child that liked to eat paste. He missed his first two class periods, social studies and P.E, but his other morning classes peeled away slowly. Study hall, which would have normally been Max's nap time, dragged on longer than he wanted it to. Occupational studies was, like always, a bore, and art ended too quickly.

At lunch, Maddy walked up to him with her hand out, eyes flaring with anger.

"Keys," she snapped.

The way Maddy looked at him, and the sound of her voice, caused a quiver to ripple through his body. Her malice radiated like heat waves, and the glare from her dark eyes dared him to speak, just so she could melt him into the pile of protoplasmic, spineless goo he knew he was.

Max panicked. His mouth felt dry. His cheeks reddened. He handed the keys over silently. This was one of the moments he knew he was subconsciously dreading—the one his conscience tried to warn him about, and failed. The douche bag feeling was back again.

Twenty minutes later, when Maddy returned, she threw his keys at his feet. Taylor was behind her. She had her eyes down and her arms wrapped around her chest, like she had been violated.

Max tried to think of something to say, but he was several hours too late.

Maddy cleared her throat, shoved his head against the cement wall he was standing next to, gave his broken arm a strong tug, and warned, "Don't look at her ever again!"

Max tried to protest, only to squeal in pain. He wanted to explain. He wanted to know what Taylor had told Maddy. Most importantly, a part of him wanted to sincerely apologize.

But how do I apologize to her? Max attempted to look Taylor in the eye, but she wouldn't remove her attention from the floor. *Would she even understand? Hell, I don't even fucking understand. God, did Laura feel like this when she gave me that stupid letter?*

"Don't!" everything about Maddy screamed venomous hate. She took Taylor by the hand and walked away, like a police officer escorting a rape victim to the hospital.

Max looked around the cafeteria, hoping no one noticed Maddy's outburst or Taylor's uncharacteristic meekness. *Shit,* he thought.

Lunch blurred into math like one long smorgasbord of snack cakes, candy bars, and soda—Max's lunch of choice, and finally, English, where he had to force all thoughts of his unfortunate morning with Taylor and Maddy out of his mind.

There was something far more interesting running through the gossip train at North High School. Everyone had heard, "The Dinkman Dad was dying." Max and Maddy weren't even that popular, but information like that spread like hot butter on warm toast. By seventh period, he had received a few notes from his counselor asking him to see her, but Max didn't want to talk. The idea of a heart-to-heart with Ms. Jennick, whose defining features were her blubbery kankles and bouncing booly, was nothing short of mortifying.

When the last bell rang, Max decided he didn't need the drama that would entail a trip home or a conversation with any of his friends. He was supposed to go straight home with Paul and take Moses for a walk, but he didn't. Max shot out of class like a super bullet that would only stop when it hit its intended target, and made his way to his car. Home wasn't an option. If he went there, he would be forced to think about his dad's disease or deal with Maddy, who would tell Mom about his not-quite-a-tryst with Taylor.

Mom's going to be so pissed, he thought. *Hell should just swallow me up right now.*

His oversized blue apron, complete with milk and yogurt stains, black slacks, and white button up dress shirt, were all in the backseat from the last time he had worked. So he went to Shop More Foods, for once in his life, eager to put on his apron with the red block print "S" and "M" embroidered on it. All the clerks seemed to get the joke. The managers didn't.

He parked at the far end of the lot, his car facing out toward Kimberly Road, and took a few minutes to compose himself. He opened up the brown portfolio sitting in his passenger seat and began to work on his art project. It was a series of comic books, and the one thing he threw himself into. The story was about Headbangin' Hero and the Disgruntled Youth, Max's very own twisted rock and roll version of the Justice League or the Avengers.[35] Though drawing with his left hand was difficult, and he had to concentrate in order to draw a straight line, even when using a ruler, it helped him focus and unwind. So did his *Nirvana Unplugged*[36] CD.

If only I had some Enya[37] and a big bag of weed.

After Max listened to "All Apologies" for the fourth time and sketched out a couple new panels, he turned off the Metro. He gathered his work clothes from the back, and walked across the slushy pavement toward Shop More Foods, a store the man who hired him called "the last vestige of Midwestern Americana."

Cars crawled slowly through the slop of a parking lot. Yesterday's snowstorm's wrath had now become little more than a whimper. Autumn was like that in Iowa—white snow and frigid temperatures one day, green grass and singing birds the next. The snow was gray, black, and brown, and

---

[35] Justice League and the Avengers are the flagship superhero teams from DC and Marvel Comics respectively.

[36] Kurt Cobain is a musical genius, up there with John Lennon—seriously.

[37] Yes, Enya. "Orinoco Flow" is one of Max's best-kept secrets. But it's brilliant, especially when stoned.

had the consistency of human waste. People were struggling with their loaded carts. They forced them through the occasional spots of soft ice, and shook them violently when too much slush built up around the wheels. Kids cried. Parents cursed. Elderly couples stared at the ground, and Max thought they might be wondering if crossing was worth breaking a hip. He could smell gasoline, and he didn't care what Dad said when he rode his motorcycle, it stunk. The scene struck him as odd. The sun, which returned for the afternoon, made everything more miserable after the snowstorm.

As he neared the building, Max kept a keen eye on the human-sized red letters over the store's automatic entrance doors. He couldn't count how many times he had pictured them falling on some sorry sap who just wanted a six-pack. The building loomed before him like the tan colored stonewalls of a penitentiary, complete with ceiling to floor windows, advertisements for, "Half-price Tuesdays" in the Deli. Max noticed an ancient hippie in paint-spattered suspenders decorating Shop More Food's main windows. He was standing on a ladder with one arm stretched out, brush in hand, painting a dark red curve. Max guessed it was going to be a candy cane.

Halloween is over, he reminded himself, *bring on Thanksgiving and Christmas.*

The familiar electric noises of scanners beeping as cashiers waved various products over their little red eyes were the same as they were two days before. A steady, calming murmur swept around the checkouts. Customers opened their wallets, employees counted the cash, and shopping carts creaked leisurely down the back aisle to the drive-up lane.

Standing in the flower shop to Max's right was Gloria, the old flower lady with creases so deep in her face she looked like the back end of a rhino, wrapping a bundle of red roses. When she waved, he gave her a polite nod. To Max's left was the video rental counter where Scott worked—but he wasn't there. Max breathed a sigh of relief until he noticed a couple of customers milling around the new releases section, pretending they weren't waiting for a clerk. He turned away from them and hoped they didn't realize he was an employee. Before disappearing to the back of the store though, Max took a moment to soak in the toxic fragrance of fifty types of flowers reeling from the cold that snuck in every few seconds with each new customer.

He always liked the front of the store, but Max resigned himself to spending the next six to eight hours knee deep in nasty. The odor of stale cheese and lumpy yogurt found its way into his nose before he was anywhere near the cooler. The smell was too strong to be coming from the dirty clothes he carried with him. It was like the foul stink sensed his presence, climbed up out of some dark secret hiding spot, and clung to him while he made his way down Aisle 20: Make Up, Hosiery, Jewelry, and Hair Care.

After popping a couple of the acetaminophen for his arm, Max put on his uniform in the employee restroom. He entered the break room at the back of the store where the time clock hung, waiting to be punched. When he entered, the door swished back and forth. The room became quiet. Everyone looked up from the television, their magazines, or their conversations. Max heard the music from *The Good, The Bad, and The Ugly* again and wished he was as badass as Clint Eastwood.[38]

A few people broke into awkward smiles.

An older, pretty girl, whose name Max didn't know, patted him on the shoulder as she punched out.

"Sorry," she said.

Goddamn news travels fast, Max thought, surprised. *How could they know my dad has cancer? Or did they find out Laura dumped me?*

Then another nameless day shift clerk said, "That loser who was supposed to work with you didn't show." He punched out and laughed, "Have fun, bro."

Max looked at the clock. *It's going to be a long night.*

Out of all the jobs at Shop More Foods Max had been assigned to, he hated dairy clerk the most. Sticky cheese forcing its way out of popped

---

[38] But really, who is? Clint Eastwood is the star of such classics as the aforementioned *The Good, The Bad, and The Ugly, Dirty Harry,* and *Unforgiven.* Seriously, comparing oneself to him is like asking for a punch in the face.

plastic containers and milk crates overstuffed with dairy products reminded him of *The Blob.*[39] The cleaning supplies smelled of mildew. The nightly cooler mop down was little more than an exercise in futility, and rotten milk stuck to him like cologne. Oftentimes, after spending hours in the cooler, and a congealed layer of sweat froze his insides, Max wondered if Dante had missed this level of hell when he went through it.[40]

Level 6½—the dairy cooler. Max let out a sigh, thinking this was where he belonged.

He rolled up his sleeves and punched in at 4:00pm—on the dot—a skill he had learned from his Dad: "Whatever job you have, do the best you can do, but never clock in early. Ever."

He was looking for the pallet hook so he could move the milk crates around without touching their crusted, rusty surfaces, when Scott ran through the double doors into the backroom.

"*Amigo*!" Scott cried, his smile so wide it looked like he was wearing a bleached-white bandanna over his mouth.

"What?" Max jumped back, startled. "What the fuck do you want?"

"*¿Qué te pasa?*" the enthusiasm drained from Scott's voice.

"I'm sorry, man. It's been a long day. Haven't you heard?"

"*N'hombre, ¿qué pasa?*" he shrugged.

Seriously, English. "You were at school today, right?"

"*Me cogieron por primera hora por esquipiar y pasé todo el dia en el Cuarto Negro,*" Scott explained.

"I have no idea what the fuck you just said."

"The Black Room, *hombre.*"

The Black Room was situated in the far south corner of North High, near the Special Education wing. Max had been there a couple times since his freshman year. It was a black painted cube that could hold no more than ten students, where teachers sent delinquents to be punished. There were

---

[39] The one from 1988 where it was purple and bloated with body parts, not the one from 1958 with Steve McQueen.

[40] Dante Alighieri, poet and author of the epic poem, *The Divine Comedy* in which Dante himself travels through hell, purgatory, and paradise. It is epic, it is grandiose, it is violent, it is vindictive. It is awesome.

rumors that some of the faculty dreamed of one day turning The Black Room into an actual Dr. Doom-esque[41] dungeon. Max imagined some of them had gone so far as to special-order chains, cuffs, iron maidens, racks, and whatever other horrible torture device they could think of.

So why is Scott so happy? If Max had spent the whole day in The Black Room, then had to come work the evening shift at Shop More Foods, he wouldn't be full of Pentecostal glee.

"What were you in the Black Room for?"

"Skipping."

"Then why are you acting so weird?"

"Carne fresca!" Scott motioned for Max to follow him out into the aisles. They emerged through the swinging double doors into the halogen glare of the supermarket. "There's a *señorita* so hot I think your face might melt right off," he continued, taking heed of one of the owner's many rules:

> **Unless you are designated as one of the Spanish speaking cashiers, clerks, or baggers, only English is to be spoken around customers.**

---

[41] Former best friend of Reed Richards (leader of the Fantastic Four) and ruler of the small Eastern European nation of Latveria. Victor Von Doom can best be described as the antithesis of every Americanized moral belief the Western World has. Does this make him evil? Maybe. Then again, maybe he just doesn't take any shit. That's admirable.

Max knew who Scott was talking about the second he saw her. They were coming up the chip aisle when the most beautiful girl he had ever seen came into view. Her black hair shimmered in the halogen light. Her skin was like lightly sweetened coffee. Her eyes were the cliché dark and mysterious kind moms warn their sons about. Though she was petite, her curves were those of a woman, not a girl. But it was her lips that caught Max's attention the most. They were full, red, round, and wore a smile with a natural ease that spoke volumes about her personality.

She was practicing on register 20, sectioned off by friendly training signs so customers knew not to interrupt. The few other trainees standing around her looked far more lost than she had ever been. Before Max had time to wonder why he hadn't noticed her when he entered the store, she started speaking, and every other thought in his head was pushed off a cliff. Her voice was like exotic, beautiful music that made Max feel only one thing: *Good*.

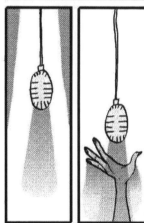

Lesson Four: Spanish II

SUGGESTED MUSICOGRAPHY

Hall and Oates—"Maneater"

Violent Femmes—"Gone Daddy Gone"

Rev. Horton Heat—"Jezebel"

Max returned to his cold cave of milk, eggs, and cheese—far away from where the new hottie was training. Customers didn't stay long in his section. It was frigid. They motored through with their screaming kids, Welfare checks, and bitter eyes, and motored out without a sidelong glance at the shaggy-haired boy behind the moving metallic wall of the cooler. The halogen lights, perpetually polished floors, Middle American smell of canned goods and bagged bread, and constant hum of Muzak tried to hide the fact that people like Max worked there, but the new trainee was different. She was a bright, shining beacon of possibility showcased at the front where everyone could see. She was Mary Jane Watson,[42] the one true love of Spider-Man's life, the one perfect girl.

Maybe I should talk to her. Max fiddled with the pallet hook as he studied the towering stacks of milk crates. He closed his eyes. *I'm not gay, damn it.*

He finished emptying the milk truck, stocking the shelves, and facing the displays early. Max paid no heed to breaks, to his broken arm under its cast begging for more pills, or to the wishes and whims of his numerous managers. People being trained always went home half-an-hour early.

At 9:00pm, Max asked Scott if he needed help opening boxes of new movies for the last hour of his shift. Max wasn't supposed to be up there with his dirty uniform on, but neither of them cared. The video rental counter was close to the practice register where the new trainee spent the bulk of her night. Max was jealous. He didn't actually help Scott, he just watched her, thinking thoughts he didn't think he should have been thinking.

Then he thought about why, *exactly,* he had left Taylor that morning. He still loved Laura—despite her recent revelations—and his dad was dying. Max was never attracted to Taylor. He hoped he could somehow push aside his feelings, but the fact was, he couldn't. Max understood now that trying to lose himself with a girl he didn't love, or even like, could never

---

[42] Mary Jane Watson is a supporting character in the Spider-Man comics who, in 1987's *The Amazing Spider-Man Annual #21* married Peter Parker, thus making Spider-Man the epitome of every comic book nerd's dream.

replace Laura, and certainly not take his mind off his dad's cancer. But Arecelli was different. He didn't know her. She was striking in a way Taylor never could be. Her physical perfection, as Max perceived it, was nearly unattainable. It was godlike. If Taylor was Calypso, then Arecelli was Aphrodite,[43] a *real* goddess. Her existence transcended the likes of Taylor and Laura. Max believed she was someone who could take his mind from the reality of his life. Someone *present,* an entity he could latch onto that wasn't his ex-girlfriend, his sexuality, Taylor, or his dad's cancer.

The realization washed over him like a warm bath.

Now I have to talk to her.

"You still eyeing Arecelli?" Scott asked, staring up at Max from a freshly opened box of new releases. "That's why you came up here to 'help?'" He did air quotes to emphasize the last word.

Max hated air quotes. He thought using them looked like something adults in suits did at business meetings.

"Her name's Arecelli?"

"*Si*, Arecelli Vasquez"

"She's hot."

"Yeah, but I heard some stuff about her tonight."

"Like what?"

"I would forget her if I were you," Scott warned. "She's a maneater like Hall and Oates.[44] What about Laura, anyway? You finally realize she gone Daddy gone?"[45]

Max chuckled. "Hall and Oates?"

"Laugh now, *amigo*," Scott bristled. Then a few strands of his dark hair, which was always styled in a perfect pompadour, slipped out of place.

---

[43] Aphrodite, the Greek Goddess of Love, Beauty, and Sexuality, grew out of the sea foam that developed when Cronus castrated Uranus and threw his junk in the ocean . . . . Yeah, that's right. The Greeks made up some crazy shit.

[44] "Maneater" is the 80s standard by Hall and Oates, with such lyrics as "She'll only come out at night/The lean and hungry type/Nothing is new/I've seen her here before . . . ."

[45] Scott is referencing another, not quite as popular 80s New Wave band, Violent Femmes, and their most famous song, "Gone Daddy Gone." Using either of these songs to define a girl equals one hell of a mess . . . .

He moved his hands and a black comb appeared out of nowhere, like magic, and groomed himself with the confident precision and deliberate ease of someone who made money off of how nice his hair looked. "Just don't come to me crying when she rips your heart out," he continued, tucking his comb away. "Bobby was in here tonight."

"Matthews? So?" Max pictured the football playing senior who grew up around the block from him. Bobby had a shaved head and eyes so beady it was impossible to tell what color they were. He looked more like a big brown mountain with a perpetually goofy smile near its peak than an 18-year-old boy. Despite that, Max liked him. Everybody liked Bobby. Being liked was Bobby's thing. "What did he have to say?"

"He came in with his *mama* after you went back to the cooler. He saw Arecelli and told me a story, man. A *story*."

"What?"

"Last year, man," Scott said, pausing for effect, "she chewed him up and spat him out. He tried to . . . uh, *suicidio*." He raised one hand over his head in a fist, and let his head fall to his shoulder, sticking out his tongue. A young mother with a cooing baby turned her cart away from the video rental counter.

"Everyone knows about that, dude. We went to see him at the hospital—me, Paul, and Maddy. Didn't you go too?" Near the end of Max's junior year, Bobby, the happy giant who was nice to everybody, was found in his parents' garage, rocked asleep by the exhaust fumes of their Ford Explorer. "I thought he was dating Alyssa."

Alyssa Beeterman, a cute, quiet girl in Maddy's grade with reddish hair, dimples, and a knack for math that had helped Max out of more than one jam in his various algebra classes, had been Bobby's girlfriend since forever, as far as Max could remember.

"Nuh-uh, they were on a break last spring, man."

"No way. He would've told me about her."

"Whatever, you guys haven't hung out since junior high."

"We hang out some . . ." Max objected, "I mean, we're friends . . . ."

"You know Arecelli goes to North?" Scott said, changing the conversation in midstream.

"No she doesn't."

"Yes she does, man, I asked her."

Max felt his fists harden again. Doomsday wanted out. *How did I miss her in the halls? How did fucking Scott, who has never had a girlfriend—who's* afraid *of girls—get the nerve to talk to Arecelli before me?*

"Anyway, her . . . relationship with Bobby," he pointed at Arecelli, "or whatever it was—was *secreto*, hush-hush stuff. It was, you know, *forbidden.*"

"You're a jackass. Why?"

"His parents are racist. *Comprende*? They think Mexicans should all go back to Mexico."

"But Bobby's black?"

"What, all black people like Mexicans now? I think you're racist."

Max crossed his arms. "I think you're an idiot."

"Whatever, man. Bobby's parents are racist. You know all the times we hung out in junior high? I never once stayed the night at his house. You did. Paul did. Even Chad did and nobody's parents like Chad. Everybody's parents like me, I'm Catholic. But his parents wouldn't let me. They're racist against Mexicans."

"Maybe that's why he tried to commit suicide?"

"Naw, he tried because Arecelli ripped out his heart—"

"And did the Mexican Tap Dance on it?"

"Keep laughing, *hombre.*"

"Okay, what did she do?" Max managed to ask through his laughter.

Scott raised his eyebrow, "You really want to know?"

"I wouldn't have asked if I didn't."

"Okay," Scott leaned in closer, as though he was about to tell a dark tale of treachery only fit for certain ears. "Word on the street—"

"'Word on the street'?" Max interrupted.

"Just listen!" Scott cleared his throat and looked around.

Max followed his gaze. When there weren't any customers in sight, Scott continued.

"So anyway, she used to go to West High, and knew she was going to come to North and wanted to be . . . I don't know . . . *cool* when she got here. Popular."

Max nodded.

"It was like in a movie or something. She knew him and Alyssa were taking a break—"

"Wait," Max lifted his hands. "How did *I* not know that Alyssa and Bobby broke up?"

"Dude," Scott smiled and shook his head, "you don't pay attention to shit unless it directly affects you."

"Wait. What?"

"Anyway, she moved in, and convinced him 110% that she loved him, was crazy about him, all that crap a sappy idiot like Bobby would go for."

"And?"

"And she lied, man. *Lied.* They had sex. She got pregnant. She got an abortion. He fell apart."

"He didn't tell you that."

"He told me some of it," Scott insisted. "The rest I heard around North, but didn't think was true until he talked to me today."

"I don't believe you."

"Whatever, *hombre.*"

A customer materialized before them and asked about a Jean Claude Van Damme[46] film. With a much-practiced smile, Scott diverted his attention from Max to find the movie.

Max looked at the clock. *It's almost 9:30. I'm going to talk to her. Laura's gone somewhere being gay. Maddy and Taylor are planning my murder. Dad is dying. I don't care if she's a maneater. I can do this!* He was

---

[46] Another action movie legend, Jean Claude Van Damme stars in such classic pieces of cinematic excellence as *Kickboxer, Lionheart, Double Impact, Street Fighter: The Movie, Universal Soldier,* and many more.

a peacock with rainbow colored feathers. He was going to strut his way over there, buy a Snickers bar, and ask her out.

But Arecelli was gone.

Max had taken his eyes away for a few minutes, but somewhere between the new releases, Bobby's story, and Jean Claude Van Damme, she disappeared. He looked at the clock on the cash register behind the video rental counter. It was 9:30pm. Her shift had ended.

***

Max walked back to the dairy cooler. When he saw the shelves could use some topping off before he punched out, he went back to work. After he wrestled a small pallet of crates into the aisle and squatted before the white shelves to begin stocking, Arecelli appeared, like a dark goddess coming down to answer his prayers. When she walked out of the double doors leading to the back room, Max stopped what he was doing and looked around. He needed a sacrifice.

Arecelli's shoulder-length black hair was shining like a shampoo commercial. Her lips were wet and Max smelled vanilla. Her white polo had one button fastened so he could see the tops of her dark, fleshy globes trying to force their way out. If they would only make it, Max knew universal peace would be declared and God would come down from heaven to begin his eternal reign.[47] The black jeans she wore were so tight around her bends and bows, that if Max focused, he thought he could make out the delicate curves of her pubic hair beneath her zipper. There was a girl standing next to Arecelli who Max couldn't see or hear clearly—but she didn't matter. He was too busy being mesmerized by Arecelli's broken English and rolling Rs, falling in love.

But then Laura appeared in his mind. Her image had always been with him before, smiling and holding a teddy bear he had won her at a winter fair when they first started dating. Her phantom scent of strawberries and cigarettes had melted his will, her voice telling him she loved him, how

---

[47] The Bible, The Book of Revelation to be exact. Not a comic book, but a surprisingly . . . interesting read.

much she cared. The feel of her skin—pampered with lotions from Bath & Body Works despite her punk rock image—had drawn him to her.

His fantasy, the one he never admitted to anyone, not even himself, was to live a long, quiet life with Laura someplace where they would be happy. He wanted to marry her, have an army of children with her, have the kind of love he thought his parents had. He wanted everything magical and cliché, deep down in the pink ruffled edges of his innermost heart—the part of him he didn't want to accept existed—the part he knew Laura knew existed.

But she left me. Probably already forgot about me.

When Arecelli turned her head and caught Max's eyes with her huge brown ones, he lost what little sense he had left. Something about big brown eyes always did it for him.

Laura had brown eyes. Max shook his head and took a deep breath. He tried to think of something clever to say as Arecelli drew closer. *But what about the girl she's with?* He panicked, swiveled on his heels, and squatted down to the shelves of milk behind him. She inched closer. Max moved the gallon jugs of white liquid around, feigning work. Now that the idea of living happily ever after with Laura wasn't possible, he began dreaming of a future with Arecelli. *I could date* her *through college, marry* her, *have kids with* her, *grow old with* her, *and die with* her, he convinced himself. His new future started building in his mind. *Oh, I'll learn Spanish!* Something he never thought about doing for Scott. *We can have a farm in Montana, or maybe Minnesota. A few acres, some place big and empty. We'll live off the grid, even if all the computers don't crash on New Year's Day, and spend all our time doing whatever it is we like to do together . . . .*

His courage came back; he was going to talk to her.

"*Excuseme,*" she said. Her voice had a tingle to it that made Max wonder if anything else ever mattered.

Still squatting, he turned to face her, staring at her black clad crotch. A normally dormant primordial part of him woke up and wanted to inhale. Lessons from health class about the male anatomy poked into his thoughts as his penis shot up with a ferocity that frightened him.

He gulped, looked up at her glowing face, and said, "Uh, hi."

Her lips bent like *Mona Lisa.*[48] Max couldn't tell if she was smiling or tolerating. She reached around his head to grab a gallon of 2%. As she did this, Max backed into the crates he had wheeled out into the aisle, and caught a glimpse of her two light brown circles of life, peaking from the confines of a pink bra underneath her barely buttoned white polo.

Of course it's pink. Max smiled to himself. *What other color would it be?* But he was smart enough not to get caught in the hypnotic beauty of her breasts. He tried to get out of her way and escape the accusatory glare of her friend. This time, since she turned away as he turned his head, his eyes happened upon her perfect backside. It was inches from his face, and she had no underwear line. *That can only mean one thing.* Max ogled the thin layer of black fabric between him and her naked flesh as she thanked him for moving.

"Gracias."

"Uh . . . *de nada,*" Max stuttered.

After an awkward, longing silence that was far shorter than Max thought, she was on her way. Max followed her hips' up and down, side-to-side motions all the way through the dairy aisle. He tried to get up enough courage to shout something to her as she moved out of sight, but he couldn't. He had failed, again.

Shaking his head at his second act of cowardice involving a woman that day, Max finished filling the shelves, returned the empty milk crates to the backroom, and punched out. Walking to his car, his coat pulled tight around him, he wondered if this meant Laura was right. His quiet mouth might have been trying to tell him something his body couldn't understand.

Am I gay?

---

[48] It's not comic book art, which naturally puts it at a #2 position, but Leonardo da Vinci's kind of smiling girl painting is eerily absorbing.

Detention Two

Wednesday November 3, 1999

Max didn't go directly home. Rather, he drove around for nearly an hour-and-a-half. For once, he wasn't worried about gas. He was sorting through his thoughts, searching for something rational to tell Maddy, Taylor, and everyone else he talked to that would explain his behavior. Eventually, Max reasoned that if he brought up Dad's cancer, whatever questions anyone might have about what happened with Taylor would fade away in an awkward, pitiful silence he would eat up if he had to. He presented his case to his conscience, which wasn't too thrilled about the morality of Max using Dad's illness to defend himself against his own stupidity. However, before his conscience could declare a mistrial, Max parked by the curb in front of his house and made his choice.

Dad's cancer is as good an excuse as any.

He found his house key and took a long look around before he stepped out of the car. The night air was hazy and frigid. Streetlights were dim and the moon was tucked safely behind the clouds, making it a movie-perfect night for a zombie attack.

Mom hadn't taken the Halloween stickers off the front house windows yet. They floated on the glass panes in strange, taunting black shapes, like tiny demons messing with Max's mind. There was a pumpkin rotting on the front porch, poking out from under a dying pile of snow. None of the house lights were on, inside or out.

Max took a deep breath. He could feel the sweat breaking out on his forehead. *Calm down. Everything's fine,* he tried to assure himself. *Zombies aren't real. They aren't going to claw open my chest, feast on my organs, and nibble on my brain . . . .* Then he bolted for the house like a trained sprinter. When Max reached the steps, his right foot caught on the bottom one, and he stumbled onto the cold, wet porch floor, dropping his keys.

"Shit," he muttered, and shoved himself up with his right hand. He bit back a cry as the pain surged from beneath his cast. "Fuck," he added, madly dashing his working hand across the slushy porch for his keys. Once he found them, he fumbled for the house key, struggling to camouflage his worry behind harsh thoughts. *They knew I was gone! What the fuck? Why is this damn light never on?*

Anytime Max was alone, outside at night, his fear of zombies took on a real quality he knew his counselor would love to hear about. His maternal grandpa had showed him a series of zombie movies when he was five. Max could remember the night his parents went on a date, his sisters had fallen asleep, and he was forced to hang out with an exotic drunk old man who was more stranger than grandfather. Grandpa, apparently, had thought it would be funny to watch his grandson go insane with terror. Max knew that was where his phobia came from. He tried to tell himself countless times that it was irrational, but the dread was too real. Nothing mattered when zombies were involved. Not Dad's cancer, Max's sexuality, or even Laura, Taylor, and Arecelli—only survival.

With every odd sound, Max's eyes darted to the bushes and toward the tree in the front yard. He mistook the pattering of loose shingles in the wind for zombified feet scraping on pavement. He heard a door open a few houses away, and wondered if a zombie was coming, or perhaps, one was chasing the last remaining member of the family down the street while the rest of them were being slowly eaten. The image of a buffet of human entrails flashed across his mind. A car drove by. He checked if the driver had any bloody bandages, exposed organs, or rotting skin—but he didn't check for long, because he knew that's when one of those undead bastards would appear from under the porch to take a bite out of him.

Once Max found the right key, got it in the doorknob—the right way— and opened the door, he froze. Mom turned the hall light on the second he had entered the house, like she had been waiting to do it all night. She stood in the entrance to the kitchen, wearing her red robe and slippers, her hair pulled back into a poorly managed ponytail.

He contemplated his chances with zombies.

"Welcome home, Maxwell," Mom said, her accent so strong Max wondered if his mother had been replaced with a character from a Mark

Twain novel.[49] "Your dad and me need to talk to you, boy." She turned around and entered the kitchen as she spoke.

Max was in trouble.

---

[49] Mom always said the only good things to come out of Missouri were the great American satirist and author of *Huckleberry Finn,* Mark Twain, and her, the great American Mother.

HEY.

YOU HAVEN'T BEEN AT WORK SINCE 11:00, BOY. I KNOW. I CALLED. iT'S ONE IN THE MORNING AND SHOP MORE'S A FIVE-MINUTE DRIVE.

NOW, LET'S TRY AGAIN.

WHERE THE HELL HAVE YOU BEEN?

UH... DRIVING... AROUND?

'DRIVIN' AROUND?' HE'S BEEN 'DRIVIN' AROUND,' BRUCE! FOR TWO HOURS! WELL THAT TAKES CARE OF THAT, DON'T IT?

TAMMY, LET HIM EXPLAIN.

YOU WANT ME TO LET HIM EXPLAIN? AFTER THE PHONE CALLS WE GOT TODAY? AFTER WHAT MADDY SAID HE DID TO POOR TAYLOR! THIS BOY DON'T DESERVE TO TALK!

YOU'RE RIGHT. BUT DIDN'T WE AGREE TO HEAR WHAT HE HAS TO SAY?

YES.

MAXWELL?

LET'S HEAR IT.

I DON'T KNOW.

NOT GOOD ENOUGH, MAXWELL.

I KNOW I SHOULD'VE BEEN HOME! I KNOW THAT!

BUT I NEEDED TO THINK.

I'M BUSTED.

I'M SORRY.

IT WON'T HAPPEN AGAIN.

DO YOU EVEN HEAR YOURSELF TALKIN'?

STOP! WE DO **NOT** HAVE TO EXPLAIN OURSELVES TO YOU! **YOU** HAVE TO EXPLAIN YOURSELF TO **US!** THAT'S HOW THIS WORKS!

BOTH OF YOU SIT DOWN NOW.

ALL WE WANT IS YOUR EXPLANATION, MAXWELL. SO GIVE IT TO US WITHOUT THE ATTITUDE.

WHY?

MADDY TOLD YOU EVERYTHING.

HE SAID WITHOUT THE ATTITUDE, MAXWELL.

FINE.

ON HALLOWEEN, LAURA DUMPED ME. I THOUGHT...

I THOUGHT...

GO ON.

I THOUGHT DOING... I DON'T KNOW... SOMETHING, *ANYTHING* WITH TAYLOR WOULD MAKE ME FEEL BETTER... BUT I CHICKEND OUT.

YOU KNOW THAT'S NOT HOW YOU TREAT WOMEN. WHY DID YOU EVEN THINK OF THAT?

SHOPMORE
MAX

WHY DID YOU LIE TO ME?

THIS CONVERSATION IS ABOUT **YOU** NOT US.

YOU'RE NOT STUPID, MAXWELL. YOU KNOW WE WOULD'VE SAID SOMETHIN' WHEN THE TIME WAS RIGHT.

Max left the kitchen without another word, but he knew his parents were holding hands and sighing to each other about his behavior. He was halfway down the hall when the bathroom door opened and Melissa emerged in all her pregnant glory. She was Eon, except without the cosmic consciousness, Protectors of the Universe, and Quantum Bands.[50] Max kept walking. He didn't want to talk to her at all.

But as he made his way down the hall, she cleared her throat and said in a snide tone, "I knew you would do something like that to Taylor."

Max stopped. "You don't know what you're talking about."

"Didn't you say that to me the other night when I told you about Dad? And didn't I know what I was talking about then? You're so predictable it's pathetic."

He sighed. "Do you want to fight with me right now? Because I'm not in the mood."

Melissa continued to berate him.

Max glared back, trying not to listen. *I'm older than her and still a virgin and she's knocked-up with a maybe-boyfriend who doesn't give a damn. Mel's reaping what she sowed,* he told himself.

Max couldn't remember a time when they were friendly. Pictures of them together from years past attested to their closeness as children. He hadn't felt it since the *Lord of the Flies*[51] island that was junior high. She had been deemed "cool" by the beast on the mountain. He had not. She had decided to join Jack and his friends in ostracizing him, and made him the butt of their jokes. But somewhere between sixth and twelfth grade, Max had made friends and became cool in his own right, while Melissa, thanks to her status as a statistic, had steadily slipped closer to the mud pit of outcast—a label she didn't wear well.

Although Max was bitter and hated her at times, he knew he should make an effort to become her older brother again, especially considering

---

[50] Eon is a cosmic entity who looks like a giant muddy green planet with a face and one roving eye. Thank you, *Quasar* (the Marvel comic).
[51] William Golding's 1956 novel about boys stuck on a deserted island, their society goes to shit.

her current situation. But not when her finger was in his face and she was yelling.

Karma's biting her in the ass for every dirty thing she ever did to anybody—to me, he thought. Max shrugged. *Fuck it.* He didn't care anymore. *If she wants to fight, fine.* Max opened his mouth, ready to tear her apart.

"GO TO BED!" Dad's voice boomed down the hallway, shaking the pictures on the walls. "*BOTH* OF YOU!"

A few days earlier, before Max knew cancer had jumped into his father, he might have challenged that dictatorial decree, but now he felt relieved. Dad sounded healthy and strong—like he was supposed to.

There would be another day.

Lesson Five: Sociology

Mom was on the phone when Max woke up the next day around 6:30am. She was speaking so loudly, her voice broke through Max's nigh-impenetrable barrier of sleep before his alarm clock could. He fumbled out of bed, scratched his head and butt, and walked toward the heated sound of her voice. Normally, Max wouldn't do this. He made it a point to avoid "Angry Mom" whenever he could—but there was a sense of distress that somehow belied her anger. He had to see what was going on.

She was pacing in the kitchen, the phone held close to her ear, as if it wanted to climb into her brain. Her grip was so tight her knuckles were as white as the phone. Her eyebrows were forced together like two gladiators in an ancient Roman coliseum. Although Max was accustomed to Mom's occasional bouts of rage, the worry that clung to her voice disturbed him.

When he caught her attention, he lipped the words, "Who is it?"

She rolled her red eyes, sniffled, covered the receiver with one hand, whispered, "Insurance," and then went back to her conversation. Her "Mm-hmms," were ferocious, rigid, and she nodded tersely as she spoke. If whomever she was talking to could see her, Max knew they would lose any collectedness they might have had, but it wasn't enough to scare him. However, the shake in her voice and the masked fear that quivered in her every word, telling him she was battling tears, did. Max saw the shaker glass on the counter filled with ice, Coke, and presumably, whiskey.

Mom tried to hide the pulsing tension radiating from her body, but Max couldn't avoid it. He was too absorbed in her broken appearance to look away. The bags under her eyes, her frizzled hair, and her dry, fatigued voice slapped him in stressful waves. Then his stomach growled—breaking his trance. With a sigh of relief, he turned away from her to open a cabinet, and pulled out a box of Cocoa Puffs. While Max filled a bowl with the cereal and some milk—concentrating as hard as he could on the task at hand because his cast loved to make everything difficult—he couldn't help but listen to Mom's half of the conversation:

"I know."

INAUDIBLE MURMURING

"No, you don't understand what I'm tryin' to say."

INAUDIBLE MURMURING

"I told you he can't work."

INAUDIBLE MURMURING

"His damn doctor, that's who!"

INAUDIBLE MURMURING

"This is what we've been payin' y'all for!"

INAUDIBLE MURMURING

"I know you're sorry! Everyone workin' at your damn devil institution is sorry!"

She hung up the phone. The dinging on the receiver sounded like a bird's final death screech after getting shot, or hit by a car, or killed by another bird.

"'Damn devil institution?'" Max asked, one eyebrow up and the hint of a smile on his lips.

"It ain't funny, Max," Mom said, running her hands through her hair. She moved to the counter next to him and flipped the coffee maker on. The solid smell of hot, Folgers Classic Roast invaded the room. With a swift wrist, Mom removed the coffee pot from the warmer and switched it with a large black mug, the phrase "#1 MOM" written in gold on the side. "Your dad might have a fightin' chance if we can get the right meds and such. But this insurance company," she shook her head, keeping her eyes on the mug, "it's like they don't want to help."

"Why were you talking to them so early?" Max asked.

"Different time zone. I thought I'd catch them first thing in the mornin,' maybe be able to talk to someone with power."

Max took his bowl of cereal to the kitchen table and began eating. "So, Dad does have a chance?" He looked out the sliding-glass door at the just-barely-there light. Moses was sitting on the back deck, staring at him. She had been acting strange for the past few days, and Max was about to ask if there was something wrong with her, when Mom's shocked voice stopped him.

"Of course he has a chance," Mom sounded as if he had just asked her what his own name was. Max watched her switch the coffee mug and the pot. She blew on the mug and walked to the refrigerator, all the while eyeing him, like she suspected he was about to sprout a second head. "You said it yourself. Your dad's tough."

Max smiled. Dad was tough—huge like a monster. He worked at a steel mill, had long hair like a lion, arms like trees, and shoulders and a chest so broad he was sometimes referred to as "Big Bad John."[52] He rode a motorcycle, had a few tattoos, and generally, people didn't mess with him. But Dad was one of the easiest going people Max had ever met. He only yelled when he felt it absolutely necessary and he was unabashedly supportive. Whenever Max showed him a picture he had drawn or a poem he had written, Dad would exclaim how wonderful his work was before even looking at it. In Dad's eyes, every effort people made to better themselves was worth a nod of appreciation. He was a good man in an old fashioned, stereotypical way, and firmly believed in family stability. He took Maddy fishing, despite the fact he disliked hearing her talk about boys and makeup and cramps. He held Melissa into the late hours of the night every time she needed comforting, especially during her pregnancy and erratic relationship with Jack. He was the rock that kept Mom sane, and the brave knight who had rescued and brought her to Davenport to live happily ever after. Dad also acted like a father-figure to Taylor when she needed one, and often invited Chad to watch football with him, even though he didn't approve of the misguided teen's weed t-shirts, saggy pants, or "smartass" attitude.

All in all, Dad was like Superman.[53] He didn't wear a cape or fly, but he brought strength and optimism to everyone around him. He did have a weakness—it seemed like cancer was Dad's green Kryptonite.[54] Max's smile faded.

"Are you even listenin' to me?" Mom's voice shattered Max's thoughts.

"What?" He looked up from his bowl, "I mean—yeah."

---

[52] Jimmy Dean's 1961 "storyteller" song about one bad mutha who saves a bunch of miners by holding up the Goddamn earth! *Big Bad John* indeed.
[53] Clark Kent, AKA Kal-El, AKA Superman, the very definition of a superhero.
[54] Superman's only weakness, the green kind can kill him.

"We're goin' to another doctor today. I have no idea what this one does . . . ." She poured some half-n-half and lots of sugar into her coffee. "I wish the damn insurance company would just cooperate."

Max stirred the chocolate milk in his bowl with his spoon. "If anybody can get the insurance to see things our way," he said, "you can, Mom."

"I hope so," she replied, and took a sip of her coffee.

The rest of the morning, Mom and Dad preoccupied themselves with insurance and medical issues. They didn't mention anything about what had happened the day before. But when Maddy woke up, she avoided the kitchen, where Max was sitting with Dad and Mom, listening to them talk about the doctor. After a few minutes, she hollered that she was getting a ride to school with Paul, and left the house without acknowledging her brother's existence. The front door slammed shut, and Mom turned away from Dad to stare directly at Max with those eyes that seemed to know everything.

She sipped her coffee, hinting a threat of bodily harm if he did not do what he was told, and said, "Apologize to Taylor today."

Max nodded. Taylor being mad at him was one thing, but Maddy was something else.

***

At school, Max's stomach bubbled and his guts twisted. He thought people were whispering behind his back, pointing and laughing as he went from class to class. But when the Dean requested Max come to his office, and they discussed why he had skipped yesterday and formally assigned him two days of in-school suspension, Max was happy. The Black Room would be a quiet place where he could avoid high school society.

Walking through the empty halls after receiving his punishment, Max thought, *I only have to make it through the rest of the day, apologize to Taylor, and see Arecelli when I go to work tonight. Then two days of peace and quiet.*

But he still hadn't apologized by seventh period. Maddy had passed him in the halls several times, stabbing him with her eyes. Taylor went in the opposite direction every time she saw him. Scott talked about how Arecelli was bad news, and Bobby helped. Paul, on the other hand, barely talked to him at all, and instead, was spending the majority of his time with Maddy. Max made a mental note to address this later. He shrugged several times in every conversation he had, and attempted to look as though he was paying attention—but the back of his mind was solely focused on the delicate situation with Taylor.

Let's see . . . Taylor, I apologize for not sleeping with you. No. That won't work. I could tell her my virginity is precious to me and I want to wait until marriage . . . . No. That's stupid. I could convince her I'm not over Laura dumping me, and that I didn't mean to be such an asshole . . . .

"Now," Ms. Deftly said, managing to take Max's attention away from his preoccupation with his shame. He looked up from his desk at her. She was wearing the same basic dress and sweater combo she wore everyday. Max often imagined she had an endless closet—that was actually a pocket universe—where she stored infinite amounts of the same dress/sweater combo in the basic blues and blacks of spinsterhood. The design had an old maid look, and on the rarest of rare occasions, she wore a flower pinned to her lapel. Nobody ever asked why because everyone feared her.

Though a woman of barely five feet, who used a cane to get from point A to point B, and did so at the pace of a two-legged turtle, Ms. Deftly commanded respect and attention. Her eyes were the color of the sky before a storm: partly blue, partly gray, and all intense. They seemed younger than her body. Her hair was done to a tee every day—slicked back into a severe, almost manly, widow's peak and white bun.

Max always pictured her as an angry Aunt May.[55] Her only goal in life was to make students miserable by forcing them to learn. She gave assignments that made them think and she placed the responsibility for success squarely on their shoulders. "Your poetry packets," she cleared her throat, "are not well." Ms. Deftly was never one to use euphemisms, which was odd, since she wanted everyone to know the meaning of the word.

---

[55] Peter Parker's (Spider-Man's) kindly old aunt who raised him after his parents died. To the best of my knowledge, she never assigned any homework.

When something sucked, she said it sucked. When people acted like idiots, she told them they were acting like idiots. When poetry packets weren't well, she told her class they weren't well.

But Max thought he had done a good job. He was enjoying poetry almost as much as drawing. The way Miss Deftly talked about and taught poetry inspired him to read his poem about Jack in class. She helped him to see the power in the right words at the right time. He wanted to be like Shakespeare, Ginsberg, Millay, Pope, and Plath.[56] He wanted his words to have power. Max thought about his fight with Jack, and how livid Jack was, and felt his words must have been pretty damn powerful.

As Max pondered the possibilities of what an "F" on his poetry packet would do to his fragile psyche, he looked around the room. He always thought English teachers were supposed to be free spirits. The kind who plastered their walls with inspirational posters, student works, and clever sayings about whatever books their classes happened to be reading. He remembered another English teacher he had in seventh grade, a middle-aged woman whose name he forgot, who had Ray Bradbury's[57] most famous quote hanging on a poster in the front of her room: "You don't have to burn books to destroy a culture. Just get people to stop reading them." Max loved that quote.

But Ms. Deftly was all business. Her desk was a study in obsessive-compulsive disorder order. Her grade book took up the front left hand corner, her plan book, the right. They were both open to the appropriate pages for the day and period. A plain white coffee cup rested on a coaster to the right of the grade book. Trays were lined neatly on the end with all the papers placed together and facing the same direction. Her "Out" pile was the only one in the building larger than its "In" counterpart. There were small 90° angles made out of masking tape on the floor, three feet apart

---

[56] Shakespeare—greatest writer ever. Allen Ginsberg—beatnik poet. Edna St. Vincent Millay—love sonnets to melt the face. Alexander Pope—genius. Sylvia Plath—distraught suicidal poet found dead with her head in an oven. Just a few of the good ones.

[57] Three words—*The Martian Chronicles*—Bradbury at his best. Also, *Something Wicked This Way Comes* . . . . so that's like eight words.

and eight feet from the front of the room. The student desks were lined based on these angles and stayed that way. Once in a while, a poster was placed on the three prison-like walls of light blue brick. Max knew it was exposed to the same regiment as the desks. The fourth wall had a lonely strip of windows that had no ability to make the room feel warm and inviting, even on sunny days. Every inch of the place smelled of pencil shavings and mints as if the old lady's aroma was imbedded in the walls.

"There are a few," Ms. Deftly continued in her clipped voice that frightened small children and animals alike, "who are doing well." She returned the work to a silent and stunned room, meticulously slapping them on desks whether or not hands or arms were in the way. Her cane thumped a slow beat with her shoes' light taps on the floor. It was the sound slaves heard in the bowels of ancient boats, paddling off to war. "Some of you understand the revision process. Some of you know the difference between copy editing and revision, and simply rewriting your work in a different colored pen." She didn't say anything else as she made her way around the room . . . slowly.

The packets were due two days ago, and there were 23 students in her advanced placement (AP) English class. Considering her agonizing, sluggish pace, Max wondered where she found the time to grade all of them. He was waiting for his impatiently, every slapping of papers and ruffling of pages made one more pore open with sweat under his armpits. His packet landed on his desk with a thud more than a slap. He wondered if it was for emphasis because his sucked so much.

This is the last thing I need, Max thought. Next to art, English was his favorite subject, the only one he got into—the only one he received 'As' in. He couldn't handle a bad grade. His belly gurgled more than it did when he stressed over Laura and Dad and Taylor and Arecelli. He looked at the rubric stapled to his pile of poems. There was no writing on it. Max wondered if he should open it and read the verdict, or shove it in his bag and look at it after work, once he had smoked some weed and turned on some mellow music, like Sublime,[58] to calm his nerves.

He took a deep breath, closed his eyes, and turned over the rubric. He scanned the first page. There were marks to go along with his, some comments in the margins, agreeing or disagreeing with what he had added, taken out, changed, or altered. No glowing words of praise or ego crushing denouncements of talent. The next page was the same. And the next, and the next, and the next. He looked up at Ms. Deftly, who was now sitting at her desk, her hands folded together atop her closed grade book.

Is she smiling? Ms. Deftly doesn't smile.

The bell rang.

"Remember your packets' next due date. Those of you who are not doing what you need to be doing to pass this class, know it. Do it next time. Have a good and productive evening."

Everyone left, even Paul, who seemed too preoccupied with the notes scribbled all over his poetry packet to be concerned with Max and his problems. Max stared after his friend, then at Ms. Deftly, anger seething beneath his skin.

"Is there something I can help you with?" Ms. Deftly asked.

Max didn't know what he wanted to say. He only knew he was angry.

"Maxwell, is everything all right?"

He nodded.

"Then what do you need? I'm a very busy woman."

Max jumped out of his seat as if he was snapping out of some enchantment. The anger evaporated and confusion set in. At that moment, Ms. Deftly reminded him of a female Dr. Strange, the Sorcerer Supreme.[59] Those who didn't know her could undervalue her power, but once they got to know her, it was clear she was not a person to be reckoned with.

"I'm sorry," he said, on instinct. "I was just wondering how I did."

---

[58] *40 Oz. to Freedom*—one of the greatest albums ever. End of discussion. Class dismissed.

[59] Dr. Stephen Strange is arguably the most powerful mortal in Marvel Comics. He is the mystical guardian of our reality. He is more than a superhero. He is more than awe-inspiring. He is a demigod.

"On your poetry assignment?" Ms. Deftly enjoyed making students repeat themselves.

"Yes," Max nodded, "on my poetry assignment. There's no grade."

"By the time one is 17 years old, Mr. Dinkman, it is a wise practice to listen to your elders and read the rubrics your teachers give you." She turned in her swivel chair toward the computer. "You'll get a final grade for the final product. Otherwise, you're doing this work to learn, not earn a grade. Read my comments. You're doing fine. Keep it up."

Max shrugged and moved toward the door. This was as good a conversation as one could have with Ms. Deftly.

She cleared her throat. "And Maxwell," she said, "I heard about your father. Keep it in mind while you're writing. Pain is a great place to begin art and . . . I hope he gets better." She didn't turn to look at him as she spoke, but Max could feel the edge of her words dull and he knew she meant it.

Is this sympathy? Max thought. He didn't like it, at least not from her. Though she was a good teacher, Ms' Deftly was stern, distant, and removed. She wasn't supposed to be sympathetic. Max couldn't handle the sudden change in her character, and left school quickly, his chest heating up and his breaths coming out in quick jabs.

I can't go home, Max thought, rubbing the tears that inexplicably sprang from his eyes the moment he sat down in his car. *I should.*

Max went to Shop More Foods.

Scott kept a spare shirt and pair of pants in his employee locker. They weren't the right fit, but Max could wear them if it meant watching Arecelli. There was a small voice in him whispering that a few glimpses of her would be just as good as the latest issue of X-Men—but there were more voices. One was yelling about avoiding Taylor, another about betraying Maddy. One vented about seeing Dad or Mom, Melissa and her big pregnant belly, and hearing her talk of how awesome Jack was. One warned him not to look over his poetry packet or his comic book from art class. Another complained about how Moses didn't deserve a walk because she had been creeping him out lately.

Though he despised working, Shop More Foods was his home away from home. The faceless people he worked with were nothing but smiles. The customers were always in need of help, and everyone at the store was there because they wanted to be. The employees, because they were getting paid. The customers, because they were shopping. It was a perfect, symbiotic relationship Max felt grateful to be a part of—even if he hated the dairy cooler. Plus, now that Arecelli was there, it was the most appealing destination he could find.

Arecelli was still training, so throughout the night Max had to come up with several reasons to find his way out of the cold, desolate dairy cooler to the front of the store. He used the bathroom a few times, bought a couple of Mtn. Dews and candy bars, and helped bag groceries whenever clerks called over the intercom for assistance at the registers. And every time he went up there, he caught Arecelli's eye and grinned. She was wearing the same saucy outfit she had on the other night. When she went on break, she passed the dairy cooler on her way to the break room. A few minutes later, Max followed, and sat at a table where she sat. She was holding an old newspaper and skimming the want ads. Max didn't want to seem like a stalker, so he kept his movements casual, and glanced around the room a bit before acknowledging her.

"Looking for another job?" he asked. Max tried to seem laid back and only interested in small talk, but it had taken him the better part of five minutes inspecting the room for possible topics. He almost started to panic before he figured out whatever she was reading would be a good place to start a conversation.

"These?" Arecelli asked. "No, I'm just, you know," she placed the paper down and sighed, not noticing how spicy Max thought her accent was. Ms. Deftly would have said she seemed exasperated.

"Busy night, huh?"

She smiled and nodded, "Training's so boring."

Max reached for the television remote, and turned on the 19 inch TV, which hung above the soda and candy machines in the far left corner of the small room. Normally, it worked in tandem with the vending machines, advertising candy bars, chips, and soda, the exact opposite of subliminal messaging. Max knew it worked just as well, if not better, because he often watched a commercial for Snickers, 3 Musketeers, or Mtn. Dew and found himself digging in his pockets for spare change. When it clicked to life this time, there was a prime time news show on about the dangers of Y2K. Max turned it off immediately.

Arecelli laughed a little, trying to stop herself.

"What?" Max asked, slightly raising his voice in mock offense.

"Why did you do that?" Her voice was chocolate dipped in sugar, then dipped in more chocolate, and served on a plate made out of candy sitting on the most comfortable bed ever made.

God's bed—that's where Arecelli sprang from,[60] Max thought. He ignored her question as he pondered what that bed might look like.

"Well?"

"I can't stand that Y2K crap," he answered.

Arecelli smiled, "Me neither." She sighed and stood up, making her way toward the Pepsi machine. "We have at least 12 more years."

"Mayan calendar," Max said, relieved he had paid attention in history class when they went over ancient South American civilizations. It was all the bloody sacrifices that had hooked him. Morbid, but cool.

After putting some change into the machine and hitting a button, Arecelli faced him. Max could see her cheeks were just the slightest bit blushed. He had taken her off guard.

Good.

"You know South American history?"

"A little," he shrugged.

"You're Max Dinkman, right?" She popped the top of a Diet Pepsi.

Oh my fucking Christ, she knows my name! "That's what people call me," Max answered, then, wanting to keep her flawless face smiling, he added, "when I'm around, anyway."

---

[60] Whereas one of Max's favorite books, *Mythology,* states Pallas Athena sprang from Zeus' head. Which birthplace is cooler?

She laughed again; it was a polite laugh, a gesture people did when someone said something that wasn't funny, but they want to keep talking anyway.

Max would take whatever he could get. She sat back down, this time at his table.

Sweet!

Then, as he studied her soda can, her expression grew serious. "Your dad has leukemia, right?" she asked.

What the fuck? "How the hell did you find out?" His response came out in a rush of tension. Max's outburst surprised him, and worse, it completely changed Arecelli's demeanor. She went from confident and flirtatious to withdrawn and quiet.

"Taylor O'Grady told me," she answered, her voice soft.

"Really," Max grunted, feeling less repentant toward Taylor. He was too riled now to calm himself down. "Why would she be talking about my dad with you? What else did she say?"

Arecelli scooted her chair away from the table and leaned back. "Nothing, really—just that your dad is a great person and, you know, it's horrible what's happened to him."

"Huh."

"This must be awful for you," she said.

"What?"

"Knowing your dad is . . . well . . . ." Arecelli looked at the newspaper on the tabletop and gently folded the corner between her forefinger and thumb.

"He's going to be fine. This morning my mom said he—" Max stopped. "You know what? Let's not talk about that, okay? I just . . ." Max felt a tremble begin in the pit of his belly. "I just can't."

"I'm sorry."

The silence could have filled up every Shop More Foods in the Midwest, the few on the coasts, and the one store in Japan. All Max heard was the clock ticking and Arecelli breathing. A sharp spasm in his arm begged for some pain pills. Before he could salvage their conversation with something friendly or witty—Arecelli stood up.

"Well, bye," she said, an awkward smile on her lips.

He nodded at her as she walked out of the room. His eyes followed, ogling her two soft-baked biscuits wrapped in tight black saran—cooling, waiting to be bitten into.

"Fuck," Max sighed, and turned the television back on. He needed something to get rid of the erection growing under his pants, but he didn't feel like jerking off in the employee bathroom. His predicament disturbed him. He wasn't sure how he could have an erection right now, especially when he was fighting so hard not to cry. On the television, a man with a camouflage baseball cap talked about how every computer was going to blow up in a matter of weeks.

Max's family didn't own a computer.

He flipped the channel. *Jeopardy* was on and it was almost over. Max laughed under his breath, thinking, *Double Jeopardy. Alex Trebek has all the fucking answers, doesn't he?*

He tried to turn the television off with the remote, but nothing happened. Max pressed the button as hard as he could and gave it a few shakes. When that didn't work, he slammed it onto the table and stood up. Before he hit the television's power button, the screen suddenly blinked, and Moses appeared—staring at him.

"Holy shit!" Max shouted. As he stepped back, he stumbled over one of the break room chairs. By the time he righted himself, and looked back at the television, Moses was gone, but something else took her place. Max couldn't breathe. His startled eyes wouldn't divert from the screen—fixated on the illuminated, appalling image presented to him.

TEENAGE ANGST

MAXWELL WAYNE DINKMAN'S FATHER DIES OF CANCER ON THIS DATE

Art Club

Thursday November 11, 1999

SUGGESTED MUSICOGRAPHY

Pink Floyd—"Comfortably Numb"

Lit—"My Own Worst Enemy"

Eminem—"My Name Is"

Max should've stopped at one joint, but Chad had handed him two after school, and told him to enjoy. Whereas Scott was avoiding the subject of Max's recent troubles and Paul was avoiding Max altogether, Chad was trying to cheer him up the only way he knew how, a way that Max appreciated.

"It's something new," Chad had told him. "My cousin brought it up from Missouri. You can be my guinea pig."

Max thanked him and drove around for hours, smoking, and waiting for Art Club to start so he could go back to school. He wanted to stop after the first joint, so he could savor the new sensation that somehow kept him tensely calm, and simultaneously relaxed and aware. But when he realized reality was seeping back into his senses, he decided to smoke all of the special weed at once—reveling in the delightful numbness it provided.

His cousin must be a fucking genius, Max thought, compliments whirling around in his head on his journey back to North High School.

When he arrived for Art Club 45 minutes early, Max took a seat in one of the empty chairs and tried to prolong his impressive high. His brain felt like it was sagging inside his skull, eyes so dry he kept repeating the familiar process of dripping Visine into them. He was toasty too, like the weed had wrapped him in a tight embrace. The notion took him back to his childhood, when everything was slower, summer break was forever, school days lasted longer, and Christmas never got here.

Max needed a break. Nothing was right anymore and it had been a long week. He hadn't bought a comic book in 15 days or drawn much. Even with his right arm broken, he knew he should have been doing something artistic, or he would be out of practice when the cast came off. Since his talk with Arecelli in the break room, though, he couldn't get himself into it at all. His abandoned poetry packet was lying next to the television in his room—gathering dust. Max's thoughts were so preoccupied that his other grades were plummeting as well.

One week is all it fucking takes, he had grumbled to himself whenever his teachers pulled him aside, and gave him a progress report with a question mark next to his grade.

His grades, however, were the least of his problems. Everything seemed to have gone to hell the day Laura told him she was a lesbian and he was gay. If that wasn't bad enough, then his parents had finally decided to let him in on the secret that Dad had cancer. Melissa was still pregnant and Jack was still the father. Maddy refused to talk to him unless she needed a ride somewhere and it felt as though Paul was drifting away—so Max figured Maddy had convinced him he had done something horrible to Taylor. In fact, he had wanted to talk to Paul about the Taylor situation for a while, but hadn't been able to since Paul had basically abandoned him.

What the fuck is his problem, anyway? Max asked himself. He was tapping his foot slowly on the linoleum, his eyes closed. *He's supposed to be my best fucking friend. It can't just be Taylor . . . can it?*

"Taylor," Max groaned. He had tried and failed to apologize to her several times. He had even managed to approach her once, but slunk away at the last minute, thinking it would be better to go home, a place he didn't like anymore.

Over the past week, Max felt like his home had transformed into something cold and lonely. Mom and Dad were always gone at doctor's appointments. Both of his sisters hated him, and whenever he was alone with Moses, he got the feeling the dog couldn't stand him. Any excuse to get him away from the house was a good excuse. So far, Shop More Foods was his best option, mostly because it paid him to be there. He could always use more money for comics and gas since he spent most of the time he wasn't working aimlessly driving around.

Max tapped an art pencil on the top of his table. He began to wonder why his life had dived into a vat of toxic chemicals, ala Jack Napier's big fall in *Batman*,[61] when he heard muffled voices coming down the hall. It was Paul, Maddy . . . and Taylor.

---

[61] In the 1989 *Batman* movie by the incomparably strange Tim Burton, Jack Napier is the Joker's name, before falling into a vat of chemicals that horribly disfigured him, drove him insane, and turned him from an ordinary wiseguy into a sociopath. Fucking brilliant.

Shit, he thought, unable to process the fact that he had just aligned himself with not just a super villain, but a super villain named Jack, something he was not prone or proud to do.

He stood and scanned the room for a place to hide. It was cavernous, but well lit, chaotic, yet organized, and filled with more art supplies than anyone would ever need. He couldn't hide behind the three huge graffiti style paintings drying on their easels. The giant yellow cabinets that lined the wall closest to the hall were stuffed with removable drawers. The door to the art office was locked. The door to the courtyard was locked. Even if he could get in there the windows looked out into a well-lit, mushy, muddy, dead grass, and snow piled mess.

Shit. Max's head was spinning like he was drunk.

His arms and legs felt like anchors—unable to move fast, or at all. The voices were getting closer. The lights felt brighter than normal. He needed to get out of there.

Shit.

"Somebody's already here," he heard Paul say as the heavy wooden door opened with a drawn-out creak.

Max was standing in the center of the room. His arms were spread, his palms were out, and he was almost crouched, as though he was going to hide by blending into the dark square tiles on the floor.

"Oh, hey," he said, trying and failing to look like he wasn't just determining the best escape from this inevitable encounter.

"Max!" Paul sounded surprised. Maddy and Taylor entered behind him, whatever discussion they were having vanished.

"Here!" Max said, unsuccessfully composing himself. "I mean—yeah. I'm here. Just me. Here. Me."

Maddy didn't say anything, but stood stiff with her arms crossed over her chest. Taylor turned toward the dust-covered chalkboard at the front of the room.

"Shit," Paul sighed. "I thought you had to work tonight."

Max shook his head.

Paul looked from Max to Maddy to Taylor and shook his head.

Max didn't know what to say without looking like a complete idiot. *What should I do?* He figured a moment of trauma like this would have sobered him up, but he was wrong. *Shit.*

"Fuck this," Paul mumbled, quietly. "Come on," he grabbed Maddy's hand and walked out of the art room, leaving Max alone with Taylor.

When Taylor tried to follow, Paul pulled the door shut behind him. The sound of that giant piece of wood slamming echoed throughout the room and Max winced as though he had been hit.

"Come on, Paul," Max whined. "What the fuck are you doing? I don't want to be alone in here with"

Taylor silenced him with a glare. She yanked on the door handles, but it wouldn't open. She groaned, and quickly turned back to the board. Then she started to sniffle.

Shit. Max raised his arms up and cleared his throat. Taylor stood still. Max paced. His footsteps sounded like big, empty heartbeats. "Taylor, I—" he stopped when her whole body shook as though hearing him say her name made her sick. She still didn't turn to face him. "Look," he began again, "I'm sorry, okay?"

"What took you so long?" she asked. Her voice was dead.

"It's hard to explain," Max covered his face with his left hand.

Taylor breathed out one of those contemptuous laughs people hear when they've done something stupid and been caught by someone who doesn't believe their apology.

He didn't say anything.

"Why'd you do that to me, Max?" Taylor asked. She was crying now.

Dad had told Max once that women were like geysers—they could blow at any minute, at will, and usually to their advantage. He could hear his dad's voice clearly, ringing in his head like a prophet: *"Whenever you have a fight with a woman, you'll always be standing there, looking like a jackass and feeling like a prick, and she'll be crying."*

"Well?" Taylor demanded.

Jesus. Max closed his eyes. He didn't want to deal with this right now. "I said I was sorry. My brain is all kinds of fucked up lately. First Laura, and then Dad, I just . . . ."

Taylor wiped away some of her tears. When he didn't continue, she glanced over at him. "Go on." Her voice wasn't as angry, but she was still crying.

"I just couldn't do it, okay?" Max said, frustrated. "I'm an asshole, a coward, spineless—take your pick." He took a deep breath. *If I bring up her talk with Arecelli things might get worse. I should just tell her something honest.* Max gulped. His body was tingling. "I tried to apologize sooner," he continued. "I *tried,* but I was embarrassed. I never . . . I . . . ."

She was getting impatient. "Spit it out!"

"I was freaked out!" he snapped in a hushed voice, a combination of irritation and vulnerability boiling his veins. "I never got that far with Laura, alright? I've always wanted to . . . I thought I was ready—but I'm not."

"Maddy told me Laura's gay," Taylor said then.

Max froze.

"I knew before you called," she shrugged, "but I didn't care about that, I just wanted to make you happy." A short, pathetic laugh escaped between her tears.

"Have you—"

"Have I told anybody else?" she shouted and spun around. Her eyes bulged out of her head like two green headlights surrounded by smeared black paint. "That's what you were going to ask, isn't it?" Her pale skin was flushed and her freckles popped.

Max took a step back. "Taylor—"

"Fuck you, Max Dinkman!" she shouted. "Fuck you!"

"I'm sorry," he begged, recoiling from her burst. "What do you want me to do?"

"You could go back in time and not be a dick!" She took giant paces toward him, crossing the room in far too short a time for Max to react.

Her hard hand, calloused from changing diapers, doing dishes, and taking care of her dilapidated house, popped against Max's fleshy cheek.

He didn't know a slap could be that loud. The snapping sound stretched over the entire room. As his eyes closed and watered up from pain, he pictured the scene as a comic book panel in his mind. Taylor raging, her hand stretched out, connecting, and the sound-effect image of the word SLAP! in giant red letters spilling off the page:

Max shielded himself with his arms, frightened she might slap again. Taylor's breaths were coming out long and hard through her nose. Her hands were at her sides, balled into tight fists.

Max felt like a hotplate had been shoved against the side of his face. He reached his left hand up and rubbed what he was sure would be a swollen, red welt in the morning. He fell back, leaning against one of the art tables.

"Apology accepted," she said, and then pulled on the door. This time it opened. Max heard Maddy call out Taylor's name, and the sounds of their footfalls tapering down the hall.

"Dude," Paul gasped, entering the room a few moments later, "Laura's gay?"

Max nodded. "Maddy told you?"

"No, we could hear you guys in the hall."

"Great . . . ." Max sat down. He didn't care that Paul knew. He probably would in the morning, but he didn't right now. He was just happy his friend was talking to him again. Max was still rubbing his cheek and smiling weakly when Chad showed up, poking his tiny head through the door like a crazy jack-in-the box.

"What's going on, guys?" Chad asked in his high-pitched, nasally voice. He swaggered into the room and motioned his thumb toward the hall. "Maddy and Taylor are out there having some kind of fucked up, little girl pow-wow."

Max sighed and looked at Paul.

Paul nodded, pulled a chair out for Chad, and told him everything he knew.

"So let me see if I understand this," Chad said, stood, and walked around the room like a mini-Sherlock Holmes.[62] He moved between the tables and scratched his chin as he spoke. Chad had a way of looking smarter and more imposing than he actually was. "Laura finally dumped you, told you she was gay, you called Taylor to—I don't know what—prove

---

[62] Sir Arthur Conan Doyle gave us this character, the former greatest detective in the world, and precursor to the current greatest detective in the world: Batman.

you're a man or something, and then you can't go through with it. Is that about right?"

Max's head was on the table. The cool feeling of hard plastic on his burning cheek eased the pain some. "Yes," he mumbled.

"That's some pretty funny fucking shit."

"You're an asshole, Chad," Maddy said, coming back into the room alone. She plopped into a chair next to Max and placed an arm on his shoulder. "All you guys are assholes."

"What did I do?" Paul asked, confused.

"You're a guy," Maddy said.

Max laughed and then swore. His cheek still hurt.

"She hit you pretty hard, huh?"

Max sat up. "Couldn't you hear it?"

Paul laughed. "Yeah."

"Where is she?" Max asked.

Maddy motioned toward the door. "She's still out in the hall. She'll be a minute."

"She's not going to hit me again, is she?"

"You're forgiven, Max. Don't worry about it," Maddy said, and leaned her head against his shoulder. "And thank God, I was getting sick of giving you the stink eye all the time."

"That's it? It's that simple?"

Maddy nodded.

"Seriously?" Max was incredulous. *"Seriously?"*

Maddy nodded again.

"I feel like a fucking idiot," he said.

"That's because you *are*," Chad laughed. He sat down and pulled his cell phone from his pocket.

"He is, but we still love him," Maddy teased. She patted her brother's arm. "At least now you know what happens when you take forever to apologize."

Max grunted.

"Girls are fucking weird," Chad sneered and then he looked up at Max with a sly smile. "Hey, I'm your friend and shit, but this story is better than your stupid zombie phobia. I'm telling everyone. You don't mind, right?"

"It doesn't matter anymore. Go for it." Max put his head back down on the table and muttered the word, *"ambulothanatophobia."* Nobody heard.

"Don't worry," Paul laughed, "the world's going to end in a month."

"Very funny," Max said.

"What are you guys doing here, anyway?" Chad asked, without looking up from his phone.

"Art Club," Paul answered. "What are you doing here, aside from being a dick?"

"I was making a transaction with one of Bobby's friends out in the parking lot, saw Lover Boy's car, and thought I'd come in and ask him about the joints." While Chad spoke, he placed the phone on the table and dug in the deep pockets of his oversized pants.

Max gave him a thumbs-up.

"Alright," Chad smiled. "Here, have this. I know how you like your sweets, especially after getting *hiiiiigh*." His voice went up a few octaves as he pulled a box of Nerds out of his pocket and tossed it across the table to Max.

"Thanks," Max smiled in return, and poured half of the box into his mouth. He didn't want to admit it, but he was really hungry.

"No problem. And Art Club was cancelled, dumbasses."

"What?" they asked.

"I don't even come to school and I knew that. Mr. Paglia's at the play," Chad folded his arms. "You know, the teacher who's *usually* here right now?"

"What play?" Max mumbled, his hand still resting gingerly on his swore cheek.

"The one Paul's in," Chad pointed a thumb at Paul.

"Do I look like I'm in a play right now, jackass?"

Max thought he noticed Paul glance at Maddy, though he was speaking to Chad.

"You were in it, weren't you?" Chad scratched his chin and squinted at him.

"I had to quit." He looked at Maddy again—Max knew it this time—who lowered her gaze to the table. "I had some more important things to take care of."

"Like what?" Max and Chad asked.

"None of your damn business," Paul said. "Anyway, you gave Max some joints? Where was I?"

Chad shrugged. "How should I know?" He turned his attention back to Max. "It was some good shit though, wasn't it?"

This was something Max could talk about.

Lesson Six: Driver's Education

Wednesday November 17, 1999

SUGGESTED MUSICOGRAPHY

Wyclef Jean—"Gone 'till November"

Another week had passed and Dad grew worse. Now that his cancer was out in the open, it was as if he had permission to let his illness shine. There were late night trips to the bathroom, plates filled with food he never ate. Fatigue that spread from him to the rest of the family, as though they were all infected. It became so bad, at one point Max wondered out loud if everyone should be tested for cancer. His joke didn't get a lot of laughs.

Visits to the hospital for treatment and exams became daily events. Sometimes Mom went, or Maddy and Melissa. Max never went. He didn't want to see the oncology unit, or learn any of the cancer terminology. He didn't want to know what sort of treatments Dad had to take, or how to maintain his chest IV. Max viewed his father's helplessness as unacceptable—he wanted to believe Dad was going to okay.

There was a bitter part of Max that was still angry with his parents. Max was sure Dad was going to live, so he saw no reason for them to lie to him for as long as they did. But the distance between them, birthed by Max's resentment, was hard to maintain—since Mom was working fewer hours and Dad wasn't working at all.

Max had never realized how much time Dad spent at the steel mill until all his hours were spent at home, wanting to talk. He always wanted to talk now—overly interested in Max's life. Max had valued his Dad's support before, but in small, healthy moderation. Lately, the support Dad offered his son was smothering and uncomfortable, and made Max recoil even more.

People at work and around school kept asking him about Dad, and all kinds of personal, prying questions Max didn't know the answers to. He thought about calling Laura to talk about it, or even Taylor, who had been speaking to him since last Thursday. Max wanted to talk to Maddy more than anyone, but he knew she couldn't discuss anything about Dad without crying.

I don't want to see her cry anymore. I hate when she breaks down. Max frowned. He was used to his little sister being strong, just like Dad. *t's funny,* he thought, *she's so tough out in public, but when she's home . . . she cries more than Melissa now.*

Everyone at North High School knew Laura was gay, thanks to Chad's big mouth. Luckily, people let Max be. Every once in awhile, he would catch someone look at him with a shy, sad glance, crooked, unclear smile, and mumble a reluctant, "Hello." Max wondered if the other students thought their parents were going to catch cancer from him. He would have invited a few playful jabs from the football team, or even welcomed Jack and his friends' harassment. He already had a good comeback for anything anyone would say about Laura: *Yeah, she figured after having me no other man would be good enough for her.* But he didn't receive any of the requisite high school pestering that would normally accompany the revelation that one's ex-girlfriend is gay. He almost felt it was worse this way.

His arm was beginning to itch. *I should've taken better care when showering,* Max scolded himself. He knew it was probably sore and festering beneath the cast and often let his mind wander over its symbolism.

The thought of Arecelli, though, kept Max going. Arecelli, with her dark eyes, dark hair, and dark skin that made him think thoughts he almost felt guilty about. He forced himself to apologize to her at work one night, and mended the bridge between them he so desperately wanted to build. She was coy at first, but said "hello" to him the next day at school. Max only nodded—but he knew there was a connection. Sometimes, if she caught him smiling at her, she would smile back—which Max believed was great progress. When he could focus on her, his worry evaporated in a haze of desire and fantasy. Arecelli at work. Arecelli at school. Arecelli in bed. Arecelli in the shower. Since she was friendly again, she became his muse. The thought of her and him together helped him work on his poetry and his comic book. He even turned them both in on time.

Scott gave up trying to persuade Max that Arecelli was "bad news," but still insisted he do some research on her anyway. After much digging and a few dead-end sources, Max found out Arecelli was a junior who had transferred to North High from West High at the end of last year. She mostly kept to herself, and there were several people who thought she was "a bitch." Bobby, who Max hardly knew anymore, let alone talked to, continued to warn him to stay away from her. This, of course, made Max want her more. He had always been attracted to dangerous women.

As the days ticked down toward Thanksgiving Break, Max's classes whirled by in a massive blur. He ignored his friends, his teachers, and Ms. Deftly's millionth announcement about how the final poetry packets were due when they returned after break. Aside from Arecelli, there was only on other thing Max could think about.

It was Wednesday, new comics day.

Max knew his family didn't have much money right now, and the insurance company was breathing down Mom's throat—but he didn't care. He had skipped his regular visits the last few weeks. He needed to buy a few. *Just a few.*

At the end of the school day, when he got in his car, he made a quick study of the area, looking for any teacher, security guard, or square who might bust him. Max pulled from the ashtray a bag of the new weed Chad had sold him—at a discount price—when they left school the night before, and a small glass pipe swirling with resin stains and bluish hues. He didn't bother cleaning the weed. Instead, he loaded the pipe, channeling the powers of Flash—the Fastest Man Alive.[63] Max didn't light it until he was well away from the mass of metal, rubber, and bodies that moved like tired ants out of the parking lot.

He decided to take the long way to River Rat Comics and Collectables. The back roads, mostly gravel, took him so far off course he was within walking distance of Eldridge, the small town about six miles north of Davenport. Beyond the odd farmer or other car full of weed and teenagers, it was private. The weather was nice. A hushed breeze blew over piles of dirty snow and harvested fields—leaves and crops the shade of wet black— and marijuana smoke so thick in the car, Max felt like he was driving through a cloud. His mind was at ease, and for once, free from thought.

---

[63] The Wally West Flash was always Max's favorite, which goes against most comic book aficionados' opinions that Barry Allen is the best.

Max's stereo blared Wyclef Jean's first album, *The Carnival.*[64] His shoulders moved to the beat. He hit "REPEAT" on track 10, "Gone Till November." His head bobbed and he floated in the music, wondering what types of music Arecelli listened to. When the pipe was cashed, he grabbed the beige Kangol off his dashboard, placed it on his head so his hair wouldn't blow in the wind. He rolled the window down to let the chill air flush out the car and skate across the skin of his left hand as it held tightly onto the steering wheel.

---

[64] Wyclef Jean, founding member of The Fugees, a musical genius.

The Cast

Check out The ABCs of Dinkology Facebook

Page for

The ABCs of Dinkology Trading Cards!

ABCs of Dinkology

#1 Max

ABCs of Dinkology

#2 Mom

ABCs of Dinkology *Life*

#5 Paul

ABCs of Dinkology *Life*

#6 Jack

ABCs of Dinkology
Life

#13 Ms. Deftly

ABCs of Dinkology
Life

#14 Chad

MAX

REAL NAME: Maxwell Wayne Dinkman
EYE COLOR: Brown
HAIR: Dirty blond and shaggy
HEIGHT: 5'10"
WEIGHT: 175 lbs.
AGE: 17 (07/22/82)
ETHNICITY: Caucasian, one-eighth Native American
BIRTHPLACE: Quincy, IL
OCCUPATION: Davenport North High Senior, Shop More Foods Dairy Clerk
FIRST SEEN: *The ABCs of Dinkology,* Lesson One: Social Studies
BIO: An avid reader of everything from Shakespeare to Spider-Man, Max is a true fanboy. He sometimes imagines he is a superhero. No one knows this. He suffers from *ambulothanatophobia* (a pathological fear of zombies), is an amateur comic book artist, and fancies himself a poet. Everyone knows this. His priorities, in no particular order, are comic books, books, movies, music, weed, and friends. He is a virgin. At the end of the 20th century he is gliding through life, unsure and unconcerned about his future. He can't wait to graduate and move on to bigger and better things. What those things might be, he doesn't know.
DID YOU KNOW?   Max was named after "Max" in Maurice Sendak's *Where the Wild Things Are,* and even had wolf pajamas when he was a toddler.

MOM

REAL NAME: Tamara Jean Dinkman
EYE COLOR: Blue
HAIR: Reddish-brown, long, and wavy
HEIGHT: 5'7"
WEIGHT: 136 lbs.
AGE: 34 (09/30/65)
ETHNICITY: Caucasian, one-quarter Native American
BIRTHPLACE: Hannibal, MO
OCCUPATION: Northpark Mall Ducky Burger Store Manager
FIRST SEEN: *The ABCs of Dinkology,* Lesson One: Social Studies

BIO: Mom is a strong, quick-witted woman who rarely laughs. Born and raised by an abusive mother and absentee, alcoholic half-Native American father in Hannibal's ghetto, she knows how to survive. After marrying Bruce Dinkman at 16, giving birth to Max at 17, Melissa at 18, Maddy at 19, and moving hundreds of miles from home, she has learned the hard way that life is never what you expect. Full of love disguised as tolerance for her children, husband, and little else in this mortal coil, she dreams of the day her luck finally changes and that obnoxious man from the lottery show picks her numbers.

DID YOU KNOW? Growing up, Mom loved her golden retriever, Champ, so much that she once ran away with him because her uncle wanted him to be a pit fighter.

LAURA

REAL NAME: Marissa Laura Levinson
EYE COLOR: Brown
HAIR: Brown and bobbed
HEIGHT: 5'3"
WEIGHT: 100 lbs.
AGE: 19 (04/15/80)
ETHNICITY: Caucasian
BIRTHPLACE: Cincinnati, OH
OCCUPATION: Chicago Art Institute Freshman
FIRST SEEN: *The ABCs of Dinkology,* Lesson One: Social Studies

BIO: Laura is a military brat with two parents in the army. Having moved once a year growing up, she has trouble developing connections. She hated Max when she first arrived in Davenport, but they developed a bond through art that later morphed their friendship into a strange obsessive monster teenagers call "love." As the summer after her graduation ended, Laura left for college, telling Max she still loved him and a long distance relationship would work. Max believed her, even though she refused to give him her virginity the night before she left. Eventually, Laura stopped calling and writing.

DID YOU KNOW? The reason Laura hated Max when they first met was his apparent indifference to her artistic abilities, something she wasn't used to from anybody.

MADDY

REAL NAME: Madison Eve Dinkman
EYE COLOR: Brown with thin, round, wire-rimmed glasses
HAIR: Blond, straight, and shoulder length
HEIGHT: 5'3"
WEIGHT: 111 lbs.
AGE: 15 (07/25/84)
ETHNICITY: Caucasian, one-eighth Native American
BIRTHPLACE: Davenport, IA
OCCUPATION: North High Sophomore
FIRST SEEN: *The ABCs of Dinkology,* Snow Day
BIO: The youngest of three children, Maddy leads as charmed a life as possible. She has always been the "baby" of the family, so her parents tend to get her what she wants. Luckily for them, and unlike her older sister, she is easily pleased. Aside from her love of all things cooking related, Maddy is a tomboy. She prefers the company of her brother and father to that of her sister and mother. However, as she grows into a young woman, her hard inner masculinity is quickly fading under her soft outer shell of femininity.

DID YOU KNOW? Maddy had spinal meningitis as an infant. It cost her all the hearing from her right ear and most of the sight from her right eye.

PAUL

REAL NAME: Paul Rain Nicholson
EYE COLOR: Blue
HAIR: Reddish-brown and shaggy with matching muttonchops
HEIGHT: 6'02"
WEIGHT: 200 lbs.
AGE: 17 (03/21/82)
ETHNICITY: Caucasian
BIRTHPLACE: Waseca, MN
OCCUPATION: North High Senior, Northpark Mall Hanover's Bowling Shirt Kiosk Clerk
FIRST SEEN: *The ABCs of Dinkology,* Snow Day
BIO: Paul moved into Max's neighborhood when they were both in fifth grade. The two became fast friends. Like Max, Paul is an avid reader. Unlike Max, he spends his class periods tucking away his massive frame into the back of the room so he can read while the teacher drones on. But Paul can be flamboyant. When he's in the mood, he actively participates in class, directs the discussions like no other, and aces quizzes, tests, and essays. This, naturally, allows him to sit in the back and read when he wants to.
DID YOU KNOW? Paul harbors a massive secret crush on Maddy and has since the first day they met.

JACK

REAL NAME: Jack Peter Ford

EYE COLOR: Blue

HAIR: Dark and cut close to the scalp in short, even spikes

HEIGHT: 6'2"

WEIGHT: 215 lbs.

AGE: 19 (10/25/80)

ETHNICITY: Caucasian

BIRTHPLACE: Davenport, IA

OCCUPATION: Davenport Public Alternative School (DPAS) Senior

FIRST SEEN: *The ABCs of Dinkology,* Snow Day

BIO: Raised in an upper-middle class home with too many rooms and not enough love, Jack grew into an angry child who sought out smaller, weaker children to torment. His parents received several phone calls about his behavior throughout elementary, middle, and high school, and though they played a good game when a teacher or administrator was on the phone, they never cared much. As long as Jack was able to star on athletic teams, everything was right in their world. Unfortunately, he lost all standing in sports at North High due to his anger and ignorance, leading him to his current school.

DID YOU KNOW?   Though Jack will never admit it, his bullying stems mostly from the fact his father physically abused him until he learned how to fight back.

DAD

REAL NAME: Bruce Wayne Dinkman
EYE COLOR: Brown
HAIR: Peppered, thick, and wavy with a matching beard
HEIGHT: 6'3"
WEIGHT: 275 lbs.
AGE: 36 (10/17/63)
ETHNICITY: Caucasian
BIRTHPLACE: Norfolk, NE
OCCUPATION: Wilton Steel Works Shift Supervisor
FIRST SEEN: *The ABCs of Dinkology,* Detention One
BIO: Dad was named after a superhero. His father, a funny, hardworking man who handed down both attributes to Bruce, named him. Even though he never liked school, Bruce was always good at it. His parents were upset when he decided to forego college, marry a 16-year-old dropout, get her pregnant three times, and move from Hannibal, MO to Davenport, IA to work at a steel mill. Dad hasn't looked back since. He was wild in his youth, and still has a 1977 Honda CB 750 Chopper (complete with authentic Von Dutch pinstripes on the tank) he takes out every summer.

DID YOU KNOW?   Dad was ashamed of his name growing up. It took his son's affinity for comic books to get him to embrace it.

MOSES

REAL NAME: Mama Moses Dinkman
EYE COLOR: Black
HAIR: Black, tan, and short
HEIGHT: 2'11" (on all fours)
WEIGHT: 105 lbs.
AGE: 8 (human years) (10/27/91)
ETHNICITY: Canine-American
BIRTHPLACE: Davenport, IA
OCCUPATION: Dinkman Family Dog
FIRST SEEN: *The ABCs of Dinkology,* Detention One
BIO: Moses was the runt of the litter, her ears and tail had already been clipped, she had no papers, and she was only $50. Though the offer sounded good, Dad had second thoughts after going to the creepy house in the Westend to pick her up. A practitioner of "river voodoo" owned her. Still, his fears subsided as she became his best friend, joining him in everything from fishing and hunting trips to walks around the block. Though a little plump in her more mature years, Moses' friendly disposition and protective nature toward anyone or anything Dad cares about has never changed, making her the epitome of the words "good dog."
DID YOU KNOW? Dad originally bought Moses for Max, but Max didn't want her.

MEL

REAL NAME: Melissa Angel Dinkman
EYE COLOR: Blue
HAIR: Blond, wavy, and hangs down to the small of her back
HEIGHT: 5'7"
WEIGHT: 197 lbs. (while pregnant)
AGE: 16 (03/22/83)
ETHNICITY: Caucasian, one-eighth Native American
BIRTHPLACE: Davenport, IA
OCCUPATION: None
FIRST SEEN: *The ABCs of Dinkology,* Detention One
BIO: Compared to her siblings, Melissa has always been the most popular in school. With the high cheekbones and long, skinny limbs of her mother's father, and the fair skin and blond hair of the women in her father's family, she is also the most beautiful. Since adolescence, Melissa has looked three years older than she actually is. She used to spend most of her time at the mall with her BFFs. However, since she's been pregnant, Melissa seldom leaves her bedroom and is a shadow of her former popular, confident self.

DID YOU KNOW? Melissa and Max haven't had a conversation more than five minutes long for over five months.

TAYLOR

REAL NAME: Taylor Barbara O'Grady
EYE COLOR: Green
HAIR: Red, thick, and very curly
HEIGHT: 5'2"
WEIGHT: 106 lbs.
AGE: 15 (01/01/84)
ETHNICITY: Caucasian
BIRTHPLACE: St. Louis, MO
OCCUPATION: North High Sophomore
FIRST SEEN: *The ABCs of Dinkology,* Lesson Two: Sex Education
BIO: Taylor is the second child in a family of four daughters. Her older sister has very little to do with the family. Taylor has to take care of her two little sisters because her mom is a jobless alcoholic, and her father ran off years ago, found a rich, homely woman, and married her, effectively disappearing. Despite all this, Taylor always smiles. She enjoys volunteering in kindergarten classrooms, animal shelters, and soup kitchens. She also enjoys sex and has had several conquests. For reasons unbeknownst to most of her friends, Taylor has had a crush on Max since elementary school.
DID YOU KNOW? Taylor's father is a pedophile who claimed to be in love with his oldest daughter—this is what initiated the divorce. Taylor has never shared this information.

SCOTT

REAL NAME: Scott Emanuel Lopez
EYE COLOR: Brown
HAIR: A thick, black pompadour with Elvis Presley sideburns.
HEIGHT: 6'0"
WEIGHT: 182 lbs.
AGE: 16 (02/24/83)
ETHNICITY: Half Caucasian, half Hispanic
BIRTHPLACE: Fort Madison, IA
OCCUPATION: North High Junior, Shop More Foods Video Rental Clerk
FIRST SEEN: *The ABCs of Dinkology,* Lesson Three: Spanish I
BIO: Scott is the youngest of three children and only boy of Merna Lopez and Chad Ward. His parents never married. Scott was raised with nothing but contempt for the white man who fathered him, and subsequently all white men. Through Catholicism, his mother rose above that hate and he did too. Unfortunately, his convoluted childhood left a few marks on Scott's psyche that manifest in his pathological fear of storms. As a result of his background, Scott strives to be friendly and helpful.

DID YOU KNOW?   Scott's mother is an attractive woman in her early 40s. Max jokes about how he can't wait until Scott has to call him "Dad." Scott hates this.

ARECELLI

REAL NAME: Arecelli Maria Vasquez
EYE COLOR: Dark brown
HAIR: Straight, black, and shoulder length
HEIGHT: 5'0"
WEIGHT: 97 lbs.
AGE: 16 (03/23/83)
ETHNICITY: Hispanic
BIRTHPLACE: Davenport, IA
OCCUPATION: North High Junior, Shop More Foods new Spanish Speaking Cashier
FIRST SEEN: *The ABCs of Dinkology,* Lesson Three: Spanish I
BIO: Arecelli's father was one of the first men to bring crack-cocaine to Davenport in the mid-eighties, and one of the first to leave when the heat followed him. After he left, Arecelli's mother found a man who could provide a sense of stability, but he ended up abusing both women. Her experiences with men have left Arecelli somewhat turned off to dating. But she does, and though Max thinks she is untouchable, she is quite the opposite. Despite growing up in Iowa, Arecelli speaks fluent Spanish as well as English.
DID YOU KNOW? The main reason Arecelli works at Shop More Foods is to get out of her house and away from her stepfather.

MS. DEFTLY

REAL NAME: Zelda Jane Deftly
EYE COLOR: Blue
HAIR: Long and gray, always pulled into a tight bun
HEIGHT: 5'4"
WEIGHT: 111 lbs.
AGE: 69 (06/30/30)
ETHNICITY: Caucasian
BIRTHPLACE: Bailey Island, ME
OCCUPATION: North High English Teacher, Quad Cities Poet Laureate
FIRST SEEN: *The ABCs of Dinkology,* Lesson Four: Sociology
BIO: Zelda Deftly is an internationally recognized poet and master teacher. She has been around the world several times. She never married, but has had lovers, including famous men and women. Due to her colorful past, the administrators of Davenport Public Schools have been trying to get her to retire for years, but a clause in her contract helps her continually get away with refusing. Zelda's pride is present in every slight step. Her stare makes the most arrogant, idiotic teenager melt, and even at 69, the slightest hint of her former Hellenistic beauty occasionally shines through.
DID YOU KNOW? Fifteen years ago, Zelda had an affair with a former student the summer after she graduated high school. It was the best sex of that girl's life.

CHAD

REAL NAME: Chad Felix Scholtz

EYE COLOR: Green

HAIR: Red

HEIGHT: 5'02"

WEIGHT: 110 lbs.

AGE: 18 (08/11/81)

ETHNICITY: Caucasian

BIRTHPLACE: Davenport, IA

OCCUPATION: North High Senior, student body's Primary Pot Supplier

FIRST SEEN: *The ABCs of Dinkology,* Art Club

BIO: Chad grew up in a neighborhood where gangs ruled and crackheads roamed. He learned how to survive early. Chad was a quiet child because he knew he had to be in order to get ignored; which is what he wanted, since his mother's boyfriends were abusive in more than one way. Because of his tendency to stay out of sight, Chad lives something of an "indoorsy" life. One day, when he was home sick from school during the sixth grade, he found his mom's weed while he was looking for Christmas presents. Shortly thereafter, Chad dove into the world of illicit drug dealing.

DID YOU KNOW? Chad is gay. Only Maddy knows.

AE STUEVE TEACHES DESIGN AND FILMMAKING AT BELLEVUE WEST HIGH

AND CREATIVE WRITING AT THE

UNIVERSITY OF NEBRASKA AT

OMAHA. HIS SHORT STORIES,

POEMS, AND ESSAYS CAN BE

FOUND ONLINE AND IN PRINT. TO KEEP UP TO DATE ON WHAT HE IS DOING,

FOLLOW HIM ON TWITTER @AESTUEVE.

CHRIS SMITH IS A DR. PEPPER ADDICT. HE ALSO TENDS TO PLAY TOO MANY

VIDEOGAMES AND WATCH TOO

MANY FILMS. HOWEVER, HE TRIES

TO FIND TIME TO WRITE AND ART

AND HAS HAD VARIOUS WORKS

PUBLISHED OVER THE YEARS IN VARIOUS ONLINE AND PRINT VENUES

INCLUDING PEARL NOIR, THE BONE PARADE, AND MOST RECENTLY AT

PARAGRAPH LINE. HE IS AN ASSISTANT PROFESSOR AT GEORGIA SOUTHERN

UNIVERSITY AND LIVES IN SAVANNAH WITH HIS TAILLESS CAT, MAUDE

LEBOWSKI.